15

TALES NEVER TOLD

PARTH DUBEY

Contents

About The Author

Parth Dubey, the author of "15: Tales Never Told," is a poet and novelist born and raised in India. Drawing inspiration from the diverse people around him, Parth is a traveler at heart, having covered thousands of kilometers on his motorcycle, gathering stories from every corner.

"15: Tales Never Told" is his fourth self-published work, following the success of "Kathan: An Epitaph to Be Buried," "Another Day in Fuckin' Paradise," and "Anvi: A Blessing to a Curse." Parth sees his life as a blessing, experiencing the world in a unique way, capturing what the mind finds inconclusive and ilusive. With each word, he unravels the intricate threads of human experience, inviting readers to join him on a literary journey of self-discovery.

This book is a collection of 15 short stories that Parth penned down since he began his journey.

Foreword

"15: Tales Never Told" is a compilation of 15 stories that revolve around the human mind and emotions. These stories follow troubled individuals, almost all imaginary. There are vampires, murderous doctors, and cannibals in the stories, which are unsettling but amazing nonetheless. The darkness of the stories combined with fast-paced narratives would definitely keep you on the edge!

Preface

This book consists of all the stories I have penned down over the past few years. While these stories were mostly posted in a blog post of Wordpress, I've worked on them, rewrote them, and gave them a makeover basically. So, what can you expect from this book? Patience... at a cost!

Alongside "Kathan: An Epitaph to be Buried," I consider this book to be my most intricate creation until date. While dark, these stories connect a thread between exagerrated reality and fiction. You might question my thought structure... trust me, I'm still figuring that part out.

Acknowledgements

I would like to thank all the people who have contributed to the creation of this book, giving me inspiration in the form of their emotions and expressing their vulnerabilities to me. I want to thank my motorcycle for staying faithful to me during my journeys.

I'm grateful to the readers who continue to support me with their valuable input and are watching me develop as an author and a poet.

Additionally, I also thank Anisha Pandey for the book's cover and editing Pahaad!

Finally, once again, thank you... this life, this gift that has been bestowed upon me either by pure luck or sheer mental fortitude.

ONE

DID YOU DREAM TODAY?

The other day, I found this billboard, and it had the most vivid colors and letters, all painting a lucid dream in my mind.

"Did You Dream Today?" the billboard on the side of the national highway read, and I could swear I saw this billboard in my dream, or maybe I didn't. Perhaps I have this habit of observing weird shit. Lord knows.

So, there was this house, on the billboard, that is, covered with chocolate, and I remember thinking, "This is weird." And on top of that, the starting letter of each word of the sentence, "Did You Dream Today?" was capitalized. I thought, "Why so?" And the "D" from "Dream" stood out; the designer of the advertisement did know what they were selling.

Well, it is now not a surprise that the billboard piqued my interest, and I swear to God I tried to keep my head straight and not observe weird shit... but I fail every time. Before this billboard, I was fixated on this blue gate that guarded a neighborhood house. Whatever happened to that gate?

Each day, I would go to my office via the same route and see this big-ass billboard with a huge house, and I still fail to understand what the fuck the designer was trying to promote. It was a bother, though, to look at this billboard standing in the sun and taking in the scorching heat. So one fine day, I located a tea shop that also happened to sell cigarettes.

"Sir, may I have one of your finest cigarettes and a big cup of tea with 3 cubes of sugar?" I said.

"Ah? Cubes, you say?" the owner asked.

"Oh, I mean... three spoons of sugar," I replied.

For a minute, the vendor looked at my face with a look of disgust, as if thinking, "What kind of idiot asks for sugar cubes from a roadside tea seller in India?"

"Chop, chop, c'mon now. I've got to be at the office," I said.

"A minute, sir," he replied.

"This is a fine billboard, don't you think?" I questioned.

"You're the second person who has said this to me today, and yet I fail to understand the appeal of this billboard. I think it is just something for the rich to understand. After all, there is a reason why the rich are actually rich and we are just poor, slaving off on a daily basis under the hot sun," said the tea shop owner.

"From where I stand... man, you're much richer than me. See, an average Indian drinks about 3 cups of tea each day. You sell what? 50 to 100 customers each day, considering the fact that you are on the highway. Also, during winters, I can easily triple this amount. So, based on your price of 15 rupees for each cup and side sales of biscuits, you're earning at least 2,000 to 3,000 rupees each day. That is MASSIVE!" I concluded.

"It would be wonderful if you just minded your own business and used your keen observation skills to bag a better salary," the tea shop owner replied.

I was hurt by these comments, but he was right. The only thing I've learned in life, that I do right, is observe, and yet, I haven't been able to capitalize on this skill. My brother, much younger than me, is already married and has a family, and I? I'm still a failure. There is nothing that I can look at and say, "Motherfucker, I'm proud of this!"

I see them: those who got rich by capitalizing on a talent or a skill—those who made millions selling some shit that people didn't need. This billboard is proof of that intention to sell... maybe it would be like that bitch that you so desperately want to fuck so badly, but you can't 'cause you've got a wife, and she is the one to not let you off the hook on some technicality.

Well, either it's tragic or it's true, but in my case, the truth is tragic, and it sucks, man!

So as I am sitting in front of this tea shop, eating my biscuit and having my tea, I see this stranger with a sunhat coming towards me. "This is not a beach town. It is hot, but man, this style is a bit overboard. But he does look cool, though," I thought.

There was this charm in the way he dressed, the way he talked, and his sleazy and chameleon-esque personality told me that he could sell me the story of my own life on a DVD, and I would still think it was some random movie's plot... no copyright there.

"Are you in sales, by any chance?" I asked him.

"Well, kind of, but I'm more of an 'image' creator for a brand," he said.

"Hmm... so you sell this to all the people that come to you, scamming them to buy your course or some shit? I certainly don't think you're the type to roam around in the heat, banging on doors and pleading folks to buy your weird encyclopedias and shit," I stated.

"You surely are a persistent observer, aren't you? A painful habit, of sorts, don't you think? But you see, with this new age of computers and technology coming, you are a dying breed. Your observing power and continuous yapping about how salesmen are leeches and the government is muddy, writing is for feminine men and blah blah…it is all coming to an end," he said.

"You know, there is a shop where they house computers for printing and shit…we go to this shop once every four or five months. I don't think that computers will ever be big in India… there isn't much to do. Can you buy and sell using computers, can you, sir?" I said. I was getting rattled up, you know?

"I can! That is the fucking point, and that is why you are a dying breed. Now, tell me one thing: did you see that billboard? The one with the chocolate house and shit?" he asked, seemingly agitated.

"Yep. I did. Didn't even make sense to me. What kind of idiot was responsible for it?" I confirmed.

"Well, sir, that billboard has something written in small letters near the bottom. Did your observant mind spot that?" he caught me off guard.

"I'm pretty sure you didn't. Why? Because all my life I have fought people like you… always content, your shitty regressive mindset is why you're mediocre and such values you impart to your child, who too will be spending their life like you… paying taxes and working day and night," he added.

"What is the need to bring my kids into this? I am not even a married motherfucker. Calm down! I'm not here to fight, just enjoying my tea," I told him.

"What biscuit? It is all dissolved in the cup now. Huh," he said.

And damn, I wish I had the power to restore shit into their original state or even a motherfucking strainer... so I could shove that biscuit into this sales guy's mouth, along with my cock.

"Calm down, sirs," the tea shop owner said, claiming, "I know the background both of you are coming from. You... Mr. Salesman, you are a futurist, and you, Mr. Biscuits, are more of a person with traditional values and the like. It is like a war between religion and science, and this country is already filled with enough dickheads believing in the superiority of their own fallacy and mythical strong men who went into hiding because some gold necklace-wearing old man told them to."

"Who the fuck told you to intervene?" shouted both of them at the same time.

"See, now both of you are on the same page. It is fascinating how every person comes on the same page under the influence of external factors," the tea shop owner said.

"What the fuck is he on about?" I asked the salesman.

"I wouldn't know. Maybe he's going senile with all that heat. Calling God a necklace-wearing old man, huh? What does he know?" the sales guy replied.

"Well, I apologize if I went too far with the argument," said the salesman.

I think he knew better than to come at me with irrational logic and shit. After all, the man was polite with me from the beginning, but it was me who got all excited.

"So, you're a religious person," he asked me.

"Yes! I have experienced His presence, you see, His power, during times of difficulty," said the sales guy.

"Same here, my guy," I told him.

We both shook hands and exchanged our landline numbers. He asked to pay for my tea, but I insisted on paying for both of us, and then we started moving away from each other, with the intention of resuming our days. But I forgot to ask him something, and as he was leaving, I ran towards him, saying, "Sir, what about the thing you said, that I missed on the billboard?"

"Oh, that? See, in the right-hand corner of this giant billboard, you can see something written in diminutive letters," he said.

"Yeah, I see," I replied while squeezing my eyes.

It read, "2007... and now, everything changes. The future of marketing... Join us!"

"Cool. There isn't much there, though. Did you have anything to do with this billboard advertisement?" I questioned.

"Yeah! It is an advertisement for my business. If you still fail to see anything special written in these words, then you aren't one of my customers and the desired audience," he said.

"Won't that decrease your consumer base?" I asked.

"Nope. People will soon pay top dollar for much better and intense computer-generated marketing, you'll see," he said.

I still never understood what he wanted to say. It has been years since that conversation, and I never saw that man either. Maybe his business went kaput, or maybe he died. Who knows?

I still observe shit. That hasn't changed at all. The other day, this other billboard caught my eye. It was about a car with mediocre features and a high price tag. The owner of the car had a beautiful wife, nice kids, a good house in the background, and everything was perfect!

Some advertisements just blow your mind, don't they? I wonder who is behind these clever ideas... I would pay top dollar for such a genius.

TWO

THE RECEPTIONIST

"01:00."

Yes, that is the time my digital timekeeper is showing me.

It is so dark, I can barely see anyone from the windows.

My wife used to always say, "The man who knows his inner demons and still chooses to be with them rather than relinquishing them is a man scarred for life." She isn't around anymore, but these words of hers have clung to my ears.

I miss her, though. She had a beautiful laugh, a calming voice, was great at blowjobs, and she was a real companion. Above all, she had a beautiful heart that cared for me. How did she die? When did I say she died? She got in an accident and is now paralyzed… can't speak, can't laugh, no handjobs, and definitely no input in a conversation.

She is just a memory now, and I miss her.

Well, I didn't have the heart to abandon her. Fuck, I really love her. I think right now she's sleeping quietly, and the nurse who takes care of her left at 11, and here I am, sipping this cold whiskey in my study room. I used to smoke cigarettes as well, but soon, I started getting these random coughs late at night or many times, early in the morning. I quit smoking but not whiskey because we all die in the end, don't we? Just the process differs.

So, moving onward... there is this kid, who went by the name Dave, born in Canada, who came to India for a few years to live with his grandmother. Always knew the cold mess he was. Dave's mouth had a foul stench and would always be startled by the loud exhausts of shitty motorcycles in this country. He really hated these motorcyclists... motherfucker even threw a stone at one of the riders, ended up breaking his arm and busting his legs.

An air of meaningless void always whirled around his face, as if a tall, thin, and dark tree on a cold Tuesday night. His grandmother and he lived next door to me.

The grandmother... God bless her soul, helped me a lot when my wife's condition worsened, never asking for anything in return until one day she asked me to drive Dave to his regular doctor's appointment. Now I thought it was a regular health checkup or counseling of sorts, but it wasn't.

I really don't understand, though. Why would a person do nice stuff for you and pretend to ask for nothing but in reality, they do expect you to help them whenever they are in need? I mean, fuck, man! I didn't ask you to take care of me during my wife's health issues. So, at first, I refused to help, but then she threatened to oust our secret sexual interactions. She took advantage of me!

I didn't want anything to do with that old hag, but I was horny and stressed, and so I gave in that one time! Or no, maybe two times... whatever. But she was talented at it... I mean the sucking part.

Don't be grossed out! We'll talk again once your wife gets paralyzed. Judgmental little twats!

This doctor's appointment is late at night. That's why I'm awake. I think I should drive around and wait for him to come outside. Wouldn't want him to catch a cold, or else the grandmother would be eating my ass for dinner, raw!

***

It has been two days since I went to this doctor's place. Today, once again, I had to go to the clinic. However, this was the first time I'll be driving towards a new location because the old one had caught fire, as Dave's grandmother told me two days ago, while giving me a wink and asking me to come back later and help her "do some stretching."

So, we arrived at the doctor's clinic at around 02:00 in the morning. I went inside with the kid and thought of keeping the kid some company till he waited for the doctor to call him. The environment was unblemished and clear as daylight, white as the British, as a clinic should be, and a pungent smell of jasmine saturated the air.

May 25th, 2016, the digital wall clock showed. Not many people were around... possibly because the place was expensive as fuck. We both waited. I had nowhere to be, to be honest, and my wife was asleep as well, and the gorgeous receptionist... uff. I wish I could handcuff her and go to town on her privates. You could see me drooling... on the inside.

"Dave!" the receptionist called, and it was his turn to go inside; the therapist was waiting for him. He went inside, and I slowly walked up to the girl, "Well, won't you sign me up as well?"

"What for?" she asked.

"For a date?" I replied.

"I'm married, mister!" she said.

"I ain't the jealous type. You see, I'm married as well," I said with a clever smile. "There are no other patients. Why don't we have a chat?"

"So, do you live with the kid? Is he yours?" asked the girl.

"Nope! I am his neighbor. I help him, you know, on account of him being a kid and all," I told her.

"You're the charitable type then. I like it," she flirted.

This woman's red lips seemed to call out my name. I was mesmerized every time she would say my name... I wished to bed her right at that moment, but she stopped my advances. "You know... you shouldn't sexualize women so much. We are much more than our boobs and asses."

"Completely with you on that," I said.

She likes grapes, you know. Furthermore, she had this habit of bursting her knuckles every few minutes. I wonder what that was about.

***

Dr. BJ Nath is a very renowned psychologist who helped people fight their depression, stress, anxiety, and past traumas. He was possibly one of the richest doctors in the city and even had a Porsche.

"Damn, the grandmother must be loaded!" I thought.

Well, I didn't bother much and was much more interested in taking the girl's digits, you know. So, I took them, and she asked me where I lived, and I told her... that's it. Then I left.

I knew the doctor. He had helped many of my colleagues in adverse conditions of guilt and remorse, allowing them to give themselves a second chance and not hate the person they saw in the mirror.

Personally, I find the concept of therapy useless. Others can only read your thoughts if you let them, and so, somewhere you are in control, and yes, you can heal yourself. No one from the outside has as much influence on you as you yourself. But we all need proper guidance during our dark times, don't we?

My words are starting to sound contradictory and hypocritical, aren't they? Maybe, who knows.

Dave was a very disturbed kid, I thought, after returning home. I too was once a disturbed kid, you know? Well, maybe his mind and soul have been tainted and scarred by the ghosts of his past... who knows what goes on inside the heads of others. If we did, there would be no fun in living, would there?

I met a young engineer once who recited this poem that I still remember vividly.

"Those who claim to be all-knowing,
Know nothing.
Those who know something,
Claim to know nothing.
Those who claim to not care,
Care the most.
Those who care the least,
Claim to care the most.
Those who travel to discover the self,
Are imprisoned by what others think of them.
Those who are actually discovering themselves,
Are imprisoned by humility.
If these two sides will someday meet,
The carers, the humble, and the intellects will always lose:
But there will be a victory in that."

Well... on another note, I woke up yesterday morning, didn't get to sleep even for a few hours, to the shrill voice of the nurse, and I ran towards her while losing my balance on the stairs. But I didn't fall... I have good reflexes.

Turns out, my wife died, and the nurse was crying because it was clear that the house had been robbed early in the morning, and my wife didn't leave me because of natural causes.

I went outside to call the police because there is no reception in my house, and I see that officers are already there at the neighbor's house. So, I go up to them and ask about their business and tell them mine. But then they drop the bombshell that Dave and the grandmother were brutally strangled and their house was robbed as well.

Fucking assholes.

That's it. That's my statement. Oh look... I'm smoking again... talk about plot development!

Signed... Astitva.

THREE

THE LIGHTHOUSE

His mother used to call him Adam. Yes, like the biblical character. A curious child whom you would see every now and then, riding his bike straight up to the lighthouse, 15 kilometers away from his home.

The daily ride made him lean, despite him being born as a chubby kid. His upbringing took place among the trees, the sea, and the waterfalls... He was a tropical being, never complaining about anything, engaged in his own thoughts.

On the other hand, his father was unemployed most of the time. But that did allow him the time to teach a lot to his kid and impart substantial knowledge at a very young age. The mother used to work as a maid and earn money in order to put Adam through school, while the father's duty was to put food on the table, literally... which he tried his best to do.

Also, there was this fear brewing in the heart of the mother, who didn't want her child to end up like his father. Eventually, the boy reached high school while somehow the father managed to get a job as the lighthouse keeper. At last things were starting to come on track, and there was nothing more to it.

The mother would cook the best dishes every day... a skill she was deprived of from the beginning due to lack of cash. But there is always another demon lurking near the edge of the bed, even if you change the mattress, the blankets, or the pillow covers. This demon is in relentless pursuit of your anxiousness and feeds off of it.

"The lack of bad times is a sign of the piling up of sins. Better ask our Lord and Savior for forgiveness like a true Christian does. Only then can you expect forgiveness, represented by harsh times," Adam's grandmother used to say.

"Does that mean bad times are blessings?" a young Adam asked.

"Yes. Quite true, young boy. I have high hopes for you, unlike your useless father. I spent so much of my energy on him. They used to call me the most beautiful one, and then this demon was born with the face of an angel," the grandmother said as Adam's expression turned stale.

"Oh, c'mon! I was pulling your legs. Your father isn't a bad man. He is just jobless. Look at him, cooking in the kitchen...If only his father were alive to guide him. That was a man who knew how to get shit done," Grandmother added.

"That is enough, Ma," said the father.

"Oh, pussy. If I were in your place, I would take that job at the lighthouse. But you and your superstitions... ghosts and all. I didn't raise a bitch," said the grandmother.

"Ma! Mind your words. That's my child sitting next to you," screamed the father while leaving the room and getting ready to go outside, wearing his shoes.

"You didn't have to do that," said the wife.

"Oh yes... I did. Some men need harsh words to get ahead in life," replied the old lady.

***

A few months passed, and the shifts at the lighthouse were relentless. No one wanted to take the job because of the darkness and the height of the building. Also, there was a rumor of the structure being haunted by the previous person employed there, who hasn't been found for a year.

The police tried to pin the disappearance on a local drug addict, but it turned out he was eventually ruled innocent.

"Close the case," said the Chief on account of no evidence. "This wouldn't look good."

This town is not a very big one, and every little news travels through each and every wall—moving like the raspy sound of the wind that startles the fallen leaves.

Soon, the father started staying late at the lighthouse. Sometimes, he would disappear for two or three days straight. When asked by the wife if he ate something, he would reply, "Yeah. Arthur cooked this or that for me."

On a Monday morning during the winter season, the man of the house went out to work and did not return that day. Two nights passed. Three nights passed. Four nights passed. A week passed. There was no sign of the man for weeks.

Meanwhile, the wife now started doubting her husband's commitment to their marriage and thought that he was having an affair. But this theory would also prove wrong 'cause she went to the lighthouse to check the whereabouts of the man, but he was nowhere to be found.

The police were informed, and once again, a search began, but no concrete results were found. The man Arthur did not exist. The authorities were afraid to go inside the lighthouse on account of it being haunted. The town was scared shitless of that building, and soon, it was abandoned...like a rusted iron rod, whose only use is to break someone's jaw in times of struggle.

A year passed by, and the husband was nowhere to be seen. Meanwhile, the checks from the father kept coming, but there was one less mouth to feed in the house. The lady figured that her husband left her for someone else, and soon after, the town went back to normal, and people forgot that the woman was ever married or that Adam had a father.

Soon, the time for the boy to join a college was approaching, but he didn't want to study more. He didn't want to leave town or take leave from nature's lap.

"You should study; if you get a good college and a scholarship, we won't have to worry anymore," the wife used to say.

"But Mom, I don't want it!" the boy said.

"What do you know? You're just a kid," the mother said.

After a few back-and-forth arguments, the mother agreed with Adam, saying that he won't get a penny out of her except food and shelter.

Well, the boy got a job as a waiter in a local town bar.

"What? You got a job? That is great. Now, you have to pay rent; you know that, right? So, twenty percent from your salary, I'm going to keep it," said the mother.

The grandmother was not alive anymore, and the mother was now the sole person responsible in the household. The caged bird was finally free.

Meanwhile, on his very first day of the job, Adam took off from home but never reached the bar. Nobody cared whether the boy reached the bar or not. The beers are famous for selling themselves.

On the other hand, the kid roamed around all day and ended up at the beach. There were a few shops that were closed on account of the upcoming holiday season, and a cold, pleasant air blew, sending chills down Adam's spine. The boy spent a few hours sitting on the sand, with a cigarette that he couldn't smoke, in his hand, looking at the sun bidding goodbye.

The birds were also leaving Adam alone, and soon, the sky turned dark bluish with the one or two people visiting the beach also leaving for their homes. The town wasn't famous for tourists so soon; the shops closed down, and the temperature dropped further.

The fishing boats could be seen with their nets and weird names that the owners kept for fun.

***

"'I Fish.' What kind of a name for a boat is that?" Adam wondered while looking around, and minutes later, the sky turned dark completely. As he decided to walk the path home, he saw a large cow standing in front of him, with the right horn being much larger than the left one... a tick mark of sorts.

Adam got a little anxious because of the cow and decided to start walking via a different route.

Adam walked for a decent ten minutes and somehow ended up in front of the lighthouse, and out of the blue, a thought confronted him: "The cheques from my father are addressed to my mother, so maybe my father is somewhere near with his new family and could be coming to work here."

So, the boy decided to check if his father was still working at the lighthouse. He put his right leg against the gate, which turned inside without much effort.

The boy was very curious and wanted to determine if his father had really abandoned his boy... the one whom he had taught countless things and loved so much. Well, this wasn't a day's thought, you see; it has been developing in Adam's mind since his childhood days.

But of course, writing about all that would be a lost cause… like those apples that you keep in one corner of your refrigerator, hoping that biting a rotten one once every few weeks could save you from every disease.

Well, Adam now had a sense of purpose and ran towards the entrance of the lighthouse that stood upright with its menacing presence. There was a window around the middle, and the light was switched on. Ecstatic, the boy pushed the door open and was faced with stairs that did not seem to have an end.

There was not much space in the lighthouse, which looked like it was older than time itself. It was something that Adam had never seen… so old, timeless, and scarred. The boy looked upwards and saw that the stairs continued for as far as the eye could see.

Adam decided to start climbing, and the endless ascent began. He was determined to reach the top and expected to find his father to be the person who was responsible for the light coming out of the window.

The boy was unaware of the fact that Adam's mother already knew that he did not reach the bar for work and his return to the house would be problematic.

Adam's mother, who had weaved so little dreams with the twenty percent stake in her son's salary, broke down. She had no idea that her own kid would do this to her. She was so angry and yet felt so helpless. Expectations, when not put in the right place, can kill you.

"What is this weird thing you tell me? I never raised my son to bail on responsibilities like his father. I will right this wrong, but you have to promise me that you will allow him to come to the job starting tomorrow. I will fix him," said the mother.

"I'm sorry. But now I don't trust him. I can employ him for an unimportant position with less money so that he can work and earn my trust," the bar owner said and cut the call.

The mother sat down on the ground, her back supported by the wall. She started thinking about ways to get her son the job back. After a few minutes, she picked up the phone and called the bar owner again, saying, "Hi... don't, and I repeat, don't cut the call. I would like to meet you in person, you know... to discuss... matters. I'm preparing a feast today. Tell me, sir, do you like meat? I sure do... in my mouth, against my tongue, resting on the palate of my mouth."

"See you in thirty," said the owner while removing a beautiful ring from his finger that left a faint, circular depression on the skin where it rested.

Meanwhile, Adam kept his ascent up the stairs while his mother went inside the shower, taking her entire beauty kit with her. The kid was tired, but every time he would look up, he would say, "Just a few more, soldier."

The night passed, and the dawn of a new day woke Adam up as he rested on the steps. The funny thing was that despite a new day, light failed to enter the lighthouse, and as a result, it was nearly impossible for the boy to figure out what time of the day it was. He felt trapped... and his heartbeat started to rise.

"I need to leave," he said and ran downstairs. His descent was much quicker than his ascent but yielded the same results... no end in sight.

Adam's mother woke up in the arms of the bar owner.

"Good morning, beautiful," the owner said. "Consider your debt paid. When may I see you again?"

"Honestly, you weren't bad at this. Let's say... you pick me up at five? I might even let you cum inside me today. But you have to be a good boy," said the woman while grabbing the pub owner's genitals.

"Sure, sure," he said. "Why don't you put that smart mouth to work now?"

"Let's see your performance tonight first. Impress me and I'll blow you to kingdom cum," she said.

Adam was nowhere to be found, but like his father's disappearance, no one cared. A few days later, the mother filed a complaint, and the police traced the boy's last known location at the beach, where several people saw him watching the sunset.

A team of police entered the lighthouse, climbed the stairs, searched the room with the window, which was miraculously open, and other locations, but Adam was nowhere to be found.

The entire team of police came to the conclusion that Adam fell off through the window, into the gigantic water body, and drowned... possibly eaten by some animal. For a few weeks, there was a ruckus in the entire neighborhood, which deemed the mother to be the one to murder the child because of her addiction to a lavish lifestyle and money.

Many even considered the mother a witch after the bar owner she was dating died in a car accident. None of the males in the town would talk to her, and soon, she was chased out of the town and had to sell all of her belongings.

As for Adam, he has been ascending up the stairs and still couldn't find an end. His knees gave up, his ankles burnt out... and yet he ascends to this day.

FOUR

4.5 Minutes

"Sit down, sit down! Or else, you'll get your ears cut," my father used to yell at me during those slightly cold mornings in our hometown on Sundays. I hated going to the barber. The patience required to sit through a haircut was arduous to maintain, and I was and still am not a very patient man.

So, years later, when I got a job and I landed up in this metropolis, the first thing I found was a barber who had zero patience, as I had. It was a difficult task to find a barber that could cut my hair in just a few minutes and even allow me to use my phone to listen to my music in between.

Each week, I would wait for my working days to pass and the weekend to arrive so that I could search for a barber in the narrow roads of this garbage city.

My hometown is a very small place with little to no traffic and has some of the best food you'll ever see. But this city that I work in is like a mixture of all the bad things that a city can have—flooding roads, constant construction, greedy people, and most of all, boring youngsters.

Since all of my colleagues and college friends arrived here, the only constant thing in their lives has been alcohol, cigarettes, and sex. They don't even do drugs right! On the other hand, me? I don't smoke tobacco, but I do like weed... I'd like to roll one right now! Alcohol is also not my cup of tea because the next day is never good.

Well, like I told you, I don't have an ounce of patience, so I'll get to the point. I talked to all of my male and female acquaintances in the city if they knew of a barber shop that had an employee who could cut my hair and beard in just a few minutes. I don't have much hair anyways, so why should I wait while other cavemen get their beard and hair done?

What? Why would you ask me that? I will get to that part soon, but can we focus right here, right now? I'm almost done rolling this joint, and I would advise you to keep rolling your camera as well!

So, I went around the city, checking out all the shops. I had a haircut every week for 12 weeks straight, and then the miracle happened. Oh shit, I forgot to add. Two weeks into my search, I had rented a cycle to, you know, go around and even made a friend—a doctor whom I'm going to call Doctor.

Now this guy had some serious shit going on in his life, but I couldn't care less. I was mostly high when in conversation with him, but this motherfucker told me about a barber that he once went to who had next to no customers due to his shop being in the corner of a humongous local market and a foul stench surrounding the place because of the meat shop adjacent to it.

"How do I get to this guy?" I asked the Doctor who replied, "Go to the market, take a right from the entrance, and keep on the same path until you see a beautiful mannequin."

"Pardon my intrusion," I said. "A a beautiful mannequin? How can a mannequin be beautiful?"

"Trust me, boy! When you see that mannequin, make a left and continue walking until you see another beautiful mannequin. This is where you make a right, and if you're looking at a tea shop, you're on the right path. I highly recommend the tea there and then, after you've had your tea, ask the owner of the shop about the barber who cuts hair in 4.5 minutes. That's it!" the Doctor said.

Well, I got what I wanted, and the Doctor said that he was going away for a brief period, and since then, I never saw him. On the other hand, I couldn't wait for my search to begin, but I was busy with office work. Now, I knew that the market would be... What? Do you want to know how I met him or not? Then please shut the FUCK UP! Please! I'm already high as hell. Don't bring me down by interrupting constantly.

I knew that the market would be crowded during the weekend, so I took a day off from the office and decided to make my way towards the market. Like he said, I took a right from the entrance, and gradually, after a half-hour walk, I found the first mannequin, and it was indeed beautiful. The divine shape of a woman—it was like a real person, a model, was standing in front of me.

I continued onwards, as told, and found the other mannequin, finally ending in front of this tea shop that barely had any customers. The Doctor was right... the tea was fucking magical. I couldn't get enough of it. After four cups, I was done, though.

"Do you know about a barber who claims to cut hair in under 4.5 minutes?" I asked the tea shop owner.

"What do you want from him?" He asked.

"Are you a little slow? What does any person want from a barber? You see, I don't have any patience, and I'm willing to pay him as much as he wants to cut my small patch of hair and beard as fast as he can," I retorted.

"Well, you're on the right path. You see this small door; open it and continue inside. He will find you," said the tea shop owner.

The small iron gate seemed feeble but was quite heavy and durable. I pushed the gate with force, and a small path was in front of me with no one coming from the other side. I wondered why, and so I asked the tea shop owner, who stood way behind me.

"Why is no one coming from the other side?" I asked.

"Well, that is a rare occurrence," said the owner.

I didn't think much of it and continued to move forward. There were two humongous walls and a small path in between, and the smell that the Doctor was talking about had gradually started to manifest. I kept moving, taking care that I didn't touch the walls because they were fucking filthy.

The walls had a blanket of *paan* and tobacco stains all over. Good that I was high.

I kept moving forward, and eventually, this chubby man with a giant smile and even bigger tummy came towards me, asking my name. I didn't tell him, though, because why should I? I'm not that big of an idiot.

It was creepy, but damn, that dude was so friendly that even your cameraman there, who's looking at me with such disgust, would like to be friends with him. I personally don't think he's from here, you know? One of the times I met him, he took me inside a little room in his shop, and I found a picture of a fucking UFO... could you fucking believe that?

What? You think I'm bullshitting you? Well, it seemed quite real to me. Fuck you!

Damn! Asshole, don't hit me, or I'll eat you up as well, and there ain't a thing you'll be able to do about it... like the others.

***

The barber and I became excellent friends. All over his shop, he had pictures hanging of his brothers, father, and uncles, all of whom had passed away. It was quite a dimly lit place, but damn, he was talented.

Even in such darkness, he pulled off the best haircuts that would look good on me. Hell, I was complimented by my crush in the office, and I even got to bang her! But I lasted only 5 minutes. I could only suck one titty. It was sad. Well, fuck her! I mean, I did... literally, haha!

What did I do with her? What do you mean? Oh yeah, of course we ate her. It was fun, you know. I had sex with her, then she started ridiculing me, teasing me about how I didn't even last for four strokes. It is hard, man! Who's going to tell these bitches that it is fucking hard to control the urge to cum? Now look what her smart mouth got her into... she's in my stomach, instead of taking my children in her stomach.

Why do you all look so horrified? C'mon, don't be so sensitive. I know what you guys want to know! Where is the barber right? I don't know. Possibly in some corner, partnered up with another tea shop owner. You can check the place I was told by The Doctor but most probably, he wouldn't be there.

While they go and search the area, why don't I continue the story? So, after a few weeks of visiting The Barber, I grew quite fond of him. He had this small patch of hair above his chin and below his lower lip, and funny fact, he also had a patchy beard, so he used to remain clean-shaven. Why didn't I think of that? Also, he had very little hair on the head, just like me!

Every time he would cut my hair, he would wear this apron, as if he's a chef or a cook. He really loved his art, you know, and there was something in him that attracted me.

On another note, do you remember the pictures that hung in the shop? The people in those pictures all looked just like him. I mean, some pictures were black and white and old, but I could swear that each and every one in those pictures looked just like him.

I was so fascinated by this barber... I still am. Who is he? A vampire? An alien? One fine day, he was cutting my hair, and his groin touched my shoulder, and I didn't feel bad. Damn! That was a fun day. Well, this became a routine number for us until a day came when I got up after he cut my hair and kissed him. He did not resist but pushed me away after a while.

"Why?" I asked.

"This can only be possible if you help me," he said.

And soon, I left my job, and together we started doing our bit, you know? Like Hansel and Gretel or Alvin and the Chipmunks. We had our own little thing going on, off-grid.

What? Could you please repeat? Ohh! Well, give me a few slices of pizza, and then I can get to the juicy part you've been waiting for.

Well, the two of your comrades left, the rest have gone to check the tea shop owner in the market, and you're left. Now that I look at you, you don't seem like a bad girl! I mean, you have that aura of a dominant partner; definitely your husband would love going to town on you.

You don't have a husband? Mama mia! If you ever need a cock to suck... I'm here.

Fuck you, BITCH! Why did you hit me? Where are you going? Uncuff me, you idiot, or I'll kill you. Don't you fucking look me in the eye! Do you even know what I'm capable of? How many people have I killed? Trust me, I've been entertaining you guys because I like you all, but if you start fucking with me or hit me, I will skin you and turn you into a beautiful mannequin.

***

Yeah, I know they didn't find him. I don't know where he is. Could be out of the country or this world. Who knows? Well, where's my pizza?

There it is!

You see, look at a slice of pizza. I love it. The flavors, the cheese, the thick crust, and the most adorable part—the cheese pull. When the Barber and I used to cook, we would make this amazing non-veg pizza that would blow your minds away. A little bit of meat, fried perfectly on low flame until it is tender and juicy. Uff, look at my mouth; it is salivating!

What meat? OUR meat! Haha...

You have been trying to figure it out, right? The missing people, the human bones, and everything. So, here comes the juicy part. Hey, you, the cameraman. Focus on me, my face, and my mouth. Look at me while I salivate.

The Barber was a fan of human meat. The meat shop was his own, and we sold, of course, human meat.

After a month of working for him as an assistant, I asked him what the fuck the smell was about. He finally disclosed to me that it was human meat. At first, I was terrified, and then he made a few dishes and explained to me how we were all cavemen and tribal and used to eat each other during ancient times.

The Barber believes that we are once again returning to our roots, giving in to our basic desires of meat, lust, and greed. He's right, you know. I'm not saying this because I've sucked his dick, no! I'm saying this because it is true. The dick part, too, you know?

****

So, they found him, huh? They found everything? The mannequins, the bodies, and all of that stuff... nice work, woman! I'm pretty sure that now we are not getting out of here, are we? Figured out so.

Well, it is not like I had anywhere to be. Bring the Barber in, and we'll answer all your stupid questions. I hope you have the stomach for it.

Wait a minute... where are you taking me? I told you, I'm not the Barber. I'm not imagining shit! C'mon. Listen to me!

FIVE

HALLOWEEN SPECIAL

It hurts, right? When the hands he used to touch my cheeks with are the ones with which he is dragging me. Yes, it hurts.

My heart is hurting more than my hair, which is reduced to a fuzzy ball under his clutches. There's blood on his fingers, bite marks on his neck, a scar underneath his right eye, and a gaping hole in his morality.

In the four years of our marriage, I never thought that this is where it will all end.

I met him at this secluded beach… famous for its rare turtles and amazing, calm waters. It was my last day in the city, and I wanted to soak all the views in, revisit the memories, and claim a new life of joy and personal growth.

This was my plan until he won my heart with surprise. You see, it was 2012, and the world had yet to go to shit… much better than it is now… chivalry wasn't dead. I had faith that men were mostly good, and here I am now, being dragged, each strand of my delicate blonde hair being subjected to such pressure that they are giving up on me.

Do you know how hard it is to grow hair? The hair that the entire world adores, every eye craves for, and so many beings fall for? The amount of effort to raise them, as if a dog, giving it water and food day by day... to see them blossom as the crown jewel of our existence. Now, it feels like someone set my head on fire.

I move my hands, move my legs... to no avail. Nobody ever heard me; nobody saw the nights I spent.

There is this bracelet on my right hand... made up of seashells, orange, pink, red, and white in colors. When I met him at the beach, I was collecting these shells but failed to acquire a single good piece, and he watched me as I failed my goal.

Then, I could see that he also started collecting these seashells, and for a good thirty minutes, he was swirling around me like a butterfly hovering above the flower... or now that I think of it, as an eagle above its prey.

"Excuse me," he said. "Would you like these? I got these 4 pairs of seashells of different sizes and colors. Maybe make a bracelet out of them or earrings... your choice."

I was mesmerized that another person took out time from his life to find something for me. We dated for a few months and then got married.

Everything was fine until a few months ago, when he went out to purchase groceries and then came home and saw me having my dinner. Out of the blue, he got agitated and started beating the hell out of me.

One punch would turn my nose red while the other would cut my upper lip. Day by day, I could see my beauty being taken away from me. I saw my eyes become dimmer, and my hands turned pale.

There were bruises as far as the eye could see, and I was kept hidden... far away from the eyes of others.

Well... I'm happy now that this is the last time his hands were touching me. I'm pretty sure that the duo that pressed my cheeks in times of sadness now sought to kill me, to berate my existence.

People usually claim that there are not many who trust in humanity anymore, and maybe it's true or maybe not. Honestly, I can't think straight; as you can imagine, I'm currently in dire straits.

No, I wasn't a fool for marrying this person who's hauling me down into my wonderland. He was so handsome, with his big eyes, heavy chest, and, of course, the nature of Archangel Michael himself... helped me overcome a lot in the beginning days.

I was like a kid in love, leaving my crutches of doubt, closing my eyes, crossing my hands, and leaping into his lap... only to find out it was stiff as concrete. It is not easy to fall in love, but it is definitely arduous to have it reciprocated.

***

We were close, you know. The sex, the food— everything was great. We also had a plan to have a kid together. Beautiful as a sunflower's blossom and delicate as its petals, yes, I was happy that we would soon have a kid. For 4 years I think I had it all.

You know every smoker won't smoke until the conditions arise wherein he has to, or the smoker or his conscious mind will tear the neural network apart. That's what happens with a vampire. Oh, I forgot to tell you about this part.

When you light up a cigarette and it catches fire, the smoke gradually rises from the level of your mouth and upwards. You see, the smoke is lighter than air itself. The white paper burns, keeping the tobacco inside, and you put it onto your lips, inhaling until the very last. This is how a vampire's thirst works.

Now, when my husband came to know the whereabouts of my existence, the night he saw me having my dinner, he banned me from human contact and stopped spending time with me. I didn't care... I knew I was a survivor... I had survived for years.

But you see, a human's blood has everything in it. The saline nature, the lies, the hurt, and the truth— every feeling from the heart drains into the blood. How can an animal's or any other being's blood even compare?

So, just like a smoker would, I too sometimes enjoyed a meal or two here and there. But about a few weeks ago, he found out about my guilty pleasure when I got out of control while talking to my neighbor.

"It is just the old neighbor," I said. "She doesn't deserve to live. God knows what she has been doing with that person with the medically challenged wife."

"That is none of your business," he said while using the back of his hand to teach me the way of the men.

Soon, we left the town and went elsewhere. As days passed, he got more violent, and the strength of the slaps increased. I had never seen him in that kind of rage.

One day, he decided to lock me up with no blood, not a single drop of hemoglobin, just chicken meat in front of me. Maybe he was hoping to turn me back into a human. I could see the pain in his eyes... seeing her beloved crave blood like an addict craves crack. He does love me, doesn't he?

Earlier today, we got into an argument about me not eating food, and he got fed up with my answers and once again used the Holy Rod to bring me to my knees. Hard to think that I used to enjoy being on my knees in front of him.

Can't a vampire date? Can't we have emotions? We love blood, so what? Do you kill lions because they hunt deer? Humans and their tendency to turn everything into a mirror image of them will never change, no matter the age.

My tongue turned into dried leaves. I have to fight for my life now. There is no choice.

***

I love her. She is my wife, and I really thought she could control her urges... you know? But she couldn't. The first time I saw her trying to eat our child, I hit her... banned her from human contact when she told me about her origin.

Soon, I thought she changed, but a few weeks ago, I saw her killing our old neighbor, a decent lady by all means. I was afraid for my life, for our kid's life, and so I chained her in a room. But this morning, my kid came close to her mother, and she... killed her. Ate her up. Her own child.

"Leave my hair, you asshole. I will kill you. I could hear footsteps, and I thought it was you. Bam! The door opened, and it was too late to realize that I killed my only daughter. She was terrified and scared shitless but immediately came to hug me as the last breath departed from her lungs. Tears were rolling down her chubby red cheeks. Kids are adorable, right? Especially when they're yours. I'm sorry," said my wife.

She used to forget, when hungry, that she had a kid whom she loved with all her heart. Hunger can turn even the most beautiful people into the Devil himself, is what I learned.

"It's not the blood that we vampires feed on like in humans; it's the emotion in the blood... it gives us a high. So, my fangs went out, and the next moment, my teeth sank deep in her neck, not giving my child a word," she confessed. "I'm sorry. We will have another kid, I promise."

You see, vampires don't have powers that they show in the movies, and this bitch will get what's coming for him... she killed my daughter, and she will make things right with her in heaven!

"I have been starving for a couple of days now. Please feed me before I start forgetting you," she said.

I dragged her by her hair, once I found that she killed my child. I will now put an end to her. Every time I tried to make her understand, she would take my words lightly and look what it cost me... fucking everything.

"Humans are way too emotional, and maybe it's because they don't get to live forever," I think. Well, it's not our fault because we are capable of love... we are capable of starving for others, for our loved ones. Not every being has that capability. Like this eternal filth that I adore.

"Say hello to my daughter up there," I said while taking out my shotgun.

"It is cold today, isn't it?" she said.

"It is.I really hope you understand why I'm doing this," I said.

"So, I guess, this is it, right?" asked my wife.

"Well, yes," I said as I pressed the trigger, blowing her head completely off.

"Happy Halloween, honey," I said and retired to my lovely house, awaiting the trick-or-treaters.

SIX

KNOCK, KNOCK

The couch in the hall made strange noises, irritating Aakash, the son of the person who owned this couch for a good seven years. This young adult in his early twenties has been trying to sleep after getting high a while ago... while the others in the house had gone to complete their daily chores.

"I'm not dumb. I'm not jobless. I'm just me. They don't understand me or my art. They just don't care. I will prove them wrong. My story will be known to the world. The man who broke from the chains of slavery of this stupid world, making his own way to stardom, a musician of supreme skills," thought Aakash.

Such heavy thoughts crowded his mind, and the noise of the couch interrupted these profound discussions that Aakash was having with himself. He couldn't take it anymore—the constant shrill noise that the couch made because he was losing his train of thought due to this unwanted interruption.

Pushed too far, probably; his mind gave up. Aakash felt like his thoughts were like butterflies; every time he tried to get one into a jar, it fluttered away. He tried a few more times to make it easy for himself to maintain this state of self-introspection and motivation but finally gave up and raised his hands high up in the air, perpendicular to his body, while lying on the couch.

"What was I thinking? Umm, motherfucker! I'm going to ask my parents to get this couch replaced. But what if they ask me to contribute... fuck! I don't have any money, but come to think of it, it has always been their fault that I'm such a screw-up. All the money they had, they poured into the lives of their firstborn, and here I am, left with nothing," Aakash thought.

Aakash's sister, Pari, was two years older than him and was another weird character that I can't possibly discuss at the moment. Reason? You see, writers have to go in a certain mindset to write about a particular character, and this girl—the first-born—is not someone I'd like to channel. For the rest of the story, the only thing you should know is that Aakash hates her voice.

***

It has been several hours, and the young man is still lying flat on his couch, wondering about how he is a creative soul but hasn't been able to create anything for years. The last song he created? Well, it was just a beat over which he put his garbage voice and idiotic lyrics. I think Aakash is just one of those people whom you meet and instantly realize that the cause of his suffering is the man himself.

Out of the blue, Aakash heard a loud, disturbing thud on his wooden door that was made from a very fine quality of wood. This door has been in place since Aakash had opened his eyes and drank milk with chocolate powder.

Being high as fuck, Aakash lost himself once again in a train of thoughts. "I've been listening to this thud for years.

People knock to get a peek inside. Knock, knock! How about a song titled 'Kock Kock'? Awesome! This is the one. I can feel it. This is the one that will make me famous and rich!"

Laziness is one of the biggest criminals out there—it cuts off your limbs, leaving you numb. An overactive mind and a dying body can only cause internal upheavals and destroy peace. This is, of course, just my take.

Aakash was left alone in the house, and he had nothing around him except some food and a little knife that lay on the floor.

He brought the knife from the kitchen to the couch to cut an apple but forgot the fruit. He has been too lazy to get up and bring the fruit, and as a result, the knife lies there with no bad intentions.

Another thud—this time louder—was heard, and Aakash was brought back to reality.

"Who could this person be on the other side of the door? Could it be the neighbor who has come here to tell my mother about him seeing me have a cigarette a few days ago? Maybe it is the neighbor or someone else? I don't want to open the door. Let it be. The person would eventually get tired and leave," Aakash thought.

I have this theory that procrastination is a set-up of events that lead up to a disaster. The knife rested on the floor, and open bottles littered the area, awaiting their closure and return to the refrigerator. The air, which felt stuck in the house, wanted to leave through any cracks that it found inside the building.

"I know what you're going to say. 'My life is like a formless cloud formed from particles of dust.' You're an exaggeration—just like a wolf is of a dog," Aakash retorted to the constant berates.

***

A few minutes later, three extremely loud knocks were heard at the door, and now, Aakash decided to go to sleep so that any person who's there on the other side could just go away. An hour and a half passed with no thud.

There is a moment when you are not asleep, but you can't feel your body as well. Everything looks so real, and yet you know that it isn't. It is just your imagination playing tricks on you. However, your heartbeat rises, and you're stuck, unable to move or say anything.

Aakash was stuck in this moment, and to his surprise, a final thud was heard, and a shrill, dry, raspy but debatable voice said, "Knock, knock!"

The man's mind was operating at his full capacity, but his body wasn't, and it was like he could hear, think, and do everything but wasn't able to. These few seconds felt like a day, and Aakash cursed the person behind the door for his state. Moments later, the door opens, and a fragile, old man, who seemed like a kind of a beggar, wearing a big turban, a yellow scarf, and an orange shirt with years of filth stuck on it, stepped forward.

The man's stature was diminutive, but his steps were wide and heavy. He had a huge beard and long hair, with scars all over his chest that seemed to be wounds. This ghost of a man started moving in the direction of Aakash, with each right step accompanied by a stick touching the ground.

Slowly, Aakash's fingers started to move and then his arm and legs began working as well.

Aakash sat up and asked the old man if he was crazy, banging doors in the middle of a warm, crazy, and unbearable afternoon.

"I don't have any money to give off to crazy old hags, and I definitely think that you need a doctor or you will die,"

Aakash said.

The old man was expressionless for a while, then looked behind his back and saw two people running outside the door with two giant bags loaded with stolen stuff. Aakash, too, watched them with helpless eyes, finally realizing who confronted him.

After fits of uninhibited and sudden laughter, the old man replied, "You do realize that I'm not a beggar but just a collector, and I've come here to collect."

Aakash was discombobulated and replied unsteadily, with a stillness and hopelessness in his voice, "What the hell do you possibly collect?" The old man pushed away his stick, raising his arms, and embraced Aakash, just saying,

"Come and bring that little knife, for I'm just a collector, and the blood on that knife is debt paid."

SEVEN

"ARE YOU READY, MY CHILD?"

It's 2025... a new year celebrated throughout the world. My year kicked off with this book that I penned under the shade of countless palm trees. It is such a dark, cold, and complex night, although it's summertime. Why is that so? Oh, the air freezes me to death! I think it is because of the clinging sweat.

Moments ago, I was running, and the artist who sang in my earphone—his words still haunt me. Well, this sweat in contact with my skin reminds me of a peculiar person I met. This old man had a decaying body, bags under his eyes, pimples on his forehead, and acne on his cheeks and was anything but sweet.

While I ponder, the love of my life is sound asleep, and I would be a bad soul to wake her up and tell her this story of my strange encounter with a strange man who looked at me, eyes all backwards, as if he were a ghost.

I ignored him, but I felt threatened at the time.

"My man needed some checkup," I thought to myself and moved forward.

This was my first interaction with the man, and my happiness was already drained by his aura in the very first meet.

"He's just one of those people... don't let him get to you," I thought as I continued running. On a second note, running didn't work out for me, so I don't do that activity anymore. You can call me a coward if you want.

A few days later, I was walking along this still and peaceful path with no burden, drunk on my own power. All of a sudden, I hear a crash. The sound was so loud, it reached my ears although I had my earphones on. Then I turned around and saw two cars sitting on top of each other.

It was an instant death, not for the people in the vehicles but for a person who was jogging, meshed in between the two iron boxes. To my surprise, once again, I saw this old man near the crash, who looked at me, and our eyes met. It was weird, but there, I decided to retrace my steps because I didn't want any drama.

I turned my back on this accident, and a few steps later, I saw him again... right in front of me, smiling like a nut case. The only weapon I had was to ignore this old man's existence... which I did brilliantly.

***

Repetition is one of man's most prominent qualities, but we get bored easily too. Nevertheless, I continue to wake up the next day, same as the day before.

Same thoughts, different songs were dancing in my head, and this old fella was out of my mind. I thought, "He could be a thief or a beggar who steals from people who have an accident or something. Not a safe person to be around."

A week later, the same schedule I follow, and there, I see him again, staring at me the same way. And in front of him, a woman is gasping for air while her dog is scared for its owner's life, barking in the middle of the road at the old man.

It was disgusting, and people were rushing in. But the old guy was just standing there. I thought that the old guy was a murderer, but the woman seemed to have overdosed on some kind of drug because of the frothy saliva that started oozing moments later.

A few days later, similar events followed near the site of where two cars crashed. Now, mind you, these events did not happen in a single day... but spanned over weeks. This time, once more, a person died due to an accident.

You see, the road is renowned for its accidents because it had a blind turn and no street lights. A mirror was placed but was stolen by people on the same day. The drivers couldn't see the other vehicle or person coming during the night or day, and once again, I saw this person near the crash site.

At this point, I thought this man was a ghost or something, but the next day I saw him talking to someone. Then, I wondered how stupid I was. But, while returning from the nearby grocery store, I noticed that the man talking to the old man was dead too... crushed by a garbage collecting van.

"What the fuck is happening?" I thought about it and then decided to stop going out for a few days.

Yes, I was afraid of an old man!

A few days, I remained inside four walls, stocked my supplies because I didn't feel safe. One fine day, I stepped out because I had to receive some delivery, and I was feeling confident that the old man must've left my vicinity.

But there he was... right at the gate, waiting for my arrival.

"What the fuck, dude? Are you following me?" I asked him.

He retorted, "Are you ready, my child?"

Well, I ignored this stupid's bullshit and decided to run in front of this old man and let him follow me—if he could with his dying body.

I keep my parcel near the stairs, and I go out for a run as the old man watches me, smiling.

A few minutes into the run, I felt parched, so I turned around to look for a shop, and I found one.

"Give me a bottle of water, please," I asked the shopkeeper.

"Here," the shopkeeper said, and I paid him.

As I gulped the water down my throat, I saw the same old man, smiling.

"Come. Sit," he said while pointing his finger to a bench. "I'll tell you a story."

***

This little story is of a man who loved running, unique in his obsession with running. Now, his obsession with his step count was not his distinct characteristic; his peculiar trait was his speech.

"Please pay the pennies to the people pleading," he'd say to his employees. He was the manager of one of the largest banks in the region... had a very huge ego problem, I heard.

There was no shortage of money in his case, but everyone was irritated with the way he spoke. He was stubborn when it came to working on it too. You see, years ago, this guy had a remarkably stupid idea of forming sentences where each word would begin with the same letter. He practiced hard for this challenge, and after putting years of effort into this trait... he wasn't going to let go of it.

"Swing by my shelter on Sunday, and I'll see if something can be sabotaged," he said when a poor father asked him for a student loan for his child.

Sunday soon arrived and on his way to the manager's house, the old man is run over by the car and never seen. It happened right here... on this blind turn. It is late, but the father has yet to come home. The mother calls the son for help, who then leads a manhunt for his creator.

It turns out that the manager's car had an accident with the old man. Talk about poor luck.

Well, the wealthy have a way of getting out of shit, and this is what happened. He got out with a slight fine paid to the family... that's it.

***

"Can't justice just be wrath, at times? When you're gone, do the rules of karma still apply to you?" the old man said.

"I don't know what you're talking about," I replied.

"You do," he said. "I'm asking you again, are you ready, my child?"

"Ready for what?" I asked him.

"Justice," he said.

"Do you think that they serve pancakes? The ones waiting for me? Do you think I might be able to run there? Also, plush, pillowy pancakes paint a poetic, pleasing palette," I said, and we left through the door.

Have been here since then.

"Okay... Who's next?" said the Dark Prince.

EIGHT

MY FUCKING SANDWICH

Once upon a time, a rotten teenager had this deep desire of eating a sandwich, engraved and tattooed on the inner patches on his brain. A grilled sandwich like no other—crispy, delicious, loaded with cheese and chicken, and with lots of tomato mayonnaise.

"The one thing I never imagined was that my mind would crave something other than money, marijuana, or pussy," this teenager named Roston exclaimed. Even thinking about this sandwich made him sweat because he was really hungry and maybe a little bit high.

Believe me, I swear that I could even hear the sound that his stupid mouth would make when taking a bite of his sandwich—very clearly!

"Oh, if only I could get hold of a fucking sandwich," thought Roston, one of the very few lean and tall men that don't go about their business with an arched back, powerless against gravity.

Roston's diabolical brother, Rohan—that dumb son of a bitch—was always running around the house in his diapers and would always get what he asked for since birth.

"Do parents love their younger ones more?" Roston thought while looking at Rohan asking mother for a sandwich.

"Oh, I forgot, he is the one with the golden dick in the house. His every puny proclivity needs to be fulfilled. I asked for the same sandwich he got, mentioned it innumerable times in front of my mother, and the only reply I got was that I should stop acting like a grown-up sloth and make it myself," thought Roston.

You see, one of the most salient things in an Indian family is that you have to respect your parents, even if they submerge your head into the fucking commode—for fuck's sake! Well, it's all good in the name of character development, I guess.

"I wouldn't be here if my parents were a bit less strict or did not break open my skull when I was 12," what middle-class youngsters are taught. This may not be the case for everyone, is it?

To think that those who raised questions against societal fundamentals were termed brilliant thinkers while now they are dubbed attention seekers or controversy theorists. It is fucking crazy, damn it! Nobody did see it coming.

To think that thinkers would have to stoop to the lows of irrational stories to get their word across. To think we've thought enough and now don't need to anymore, argh!

***

"I am the strong one here, right? So, why bother? This stupid superhero lover, the kid has a sandwich, and I'm in need of one, so what's the fucking doubt? I'll usurp this sandwich from this little turd. I'll just tell him some made-up story," thought Roston.

"Hey, you red-cheeked homo, give me that sandwich, or else I'll have your soul," said Roston while picking Rohan up. "You see, I've picked you up; you're weak, you are nothing, you are a waste—you're nowhere close to Mom and Dad as I am. I share the same blood... unlike you. Now, give me this sandwich."

Meanwhile, the kid who didn't know he was messing with a hungry animal dropped the sandwich from fear.

"Shit! You dropped it? You are done now. Oh boy, your life on this wretched planet is complete. Playtime's over, kid. Now, I'll show you what it's like being a grown-up. Let me fetch my baseball bat; I'll break your legs today," said Roston.

The tall teenager went towards his room to grab his weapon while Rohan knew he was in trouble. In a useless attempt to cover up his mistake, the kid tried to pick up his sandwich, resulting in the entire filling pouring out like slippery filth from the kitchen that won't go in the garbage bag.

While returning from his room with the bag, Roston had this brilliant idea to inform his parents about what he was going to do. He moved towards the slightly open door and pushed the wooden structure towards the inside, unveiling a dimly lit room that had a weird stench coming out from it.

He could hear some strange sounds coming from the chambers. Regardless, he pushed his way in.

"Oh shit, what the fuck, Mom, Dad, what are you doing?" Roston shouted.

You see, it was regular for Roston to walk in on his mom and supposed dad sharing intimate moments. Some might even call it a deliberate attempt on Roston's behalf to see the inside of the chambers—sexual curiosity, one might call it.

It's important to mention here that Roston's mother has an affair with a fairly decent man whom the teenager considers his father. "Mom says I have many fathers to choose my idol from, and I couldn't ask for much more," Roston used to brag to his friends.

Well, I know that Roston's mom is a good fuck, so do the supposed dads, but Roston doesn't.

"He has spent more on us than your real father's entire generation would've earned in their lifetime. Did I just exaggerate? Oh, you should know he spends a lot!" The mother had the same statement for every other guy.

A broken family is like food to this world—entertainment, art, whatever you might call it—it all stems from some shit someone was slapped with when they were a child.

Well, Roston decided to keep his bat back in his room and wonder about what he just saw. He looked outside the window and thought about that girl he met the other day—the one with whom he watched eagles soar over dead fish that fishermen had brought from the river.

"She was an amazing woman," Roston thought, despite not even sharing a word with her. The eagles danced throughout the fucking sky that evening, scaling the skies, claiming their territory.

"This guy on social media says that women like men with the personality of an eagle. I guess I could've had a shot with her. Maybe the next time we meet, I will get to nail her," he thought.

Out of the blue, Roston heard the sound of a plate breaking on the floor, giving birth to pieces of porcelain.

"I think I need to see what is going on," thought Roston, and he immediately unbuttoned his pants, brought out his famished cock, and finished his business, running towards the source of the noise afterwards.

"Dad, open the fucking door. What's happening? I'm calling the police. Fucking open the door now, Dad!" Roston shouted from outside the door.

The wooden structure started to move outwards, and the temporary father came out with blood on his face.

"Where's Mom? What'd you do, Dad?" asked Roston while Rohan came around and stood beside, holding his elder brother's leg.

"Hey, you slimy turd, you're too little for this shit. Fuck off, close your room, and don't come out. Now, Dad, where is Mom, and what happened?" asked Roston.

The thing is, Roston's so-called parents have always played self-proclaimed "pranks" on the teenager to teach life lessons—they often went a little overboard with the pranks, but social media is an addiction. However, this time around, the screams were too real.

"Oh shit, is that Mom? Why is she eating a sandwich in such a situation? What is all this? Wait a minute—that sandwich was on the floor—the one she's eating. Stop her, Dad!" Roston exclaimed.

You want to know what happened next?

Well, Roston looked at his mother shoving a dirty sandwich in her mouth despite being closer to choking to death.

"Lesson 798 learned," said Roston, "Don't Ask For Sandwich."

NINE
CREATIVITY

"The topic of the debate is... 'creativity as the epitome of human existence.'" I overheard a few people having a debate a few minutes ago.

"Creativity is just a way to get attention and validation. For a dude, it is a way to catch bitches and all. Using their charmed phrases, you get their way, or else, who'd like to sleep with a writer? Most don't even have money, but they fool girls into having sex by using cheesy words," the air carried a message towards me.

What is a debate? I'd say an exchange of thoughts. But once there is an audience in that debate, shit hits the fan.

I have always believed that a person is smart, but people? People generally are dumb. What has this got to do with this story? I really don't know. Just something I had in mind I needed to get out, I guess?

"A creative mind is in the system but above it. If you don't understand, let me elaborate," said this person, a writer, I think. Yes, indeed. He was a writer, or you know what? Maybe he was a poet or a singer. I really don't know. So this writer, or whatever, had joined the debate on account of his expertise in the industry—having released four projects in just one year.

"Contrary to general consensus, creativity is not gifted. Though the age of achieving creative enlightenment can differ. The most creative is a child's mind. Away from social stereotypes, its mind knows no limits. There are no hurdles or obstructions in a child's structure of thoughts. Everything is achievable, and have you ever seen a child contemplating risks? Something that many adults would like to learn and incorporate in their lives. The child's brain knows no bounds, so what you teach it, it learns quicker," said this writer.

I think you already know that this story requires a lot of reading, but it's cool if you can hang on for a bit. Now, this writer was intensely defending his territory. He knew one thing: that creativity is just supreme and could be determined as the epitome of a human's existence.

Who's not in this guy's favor? The audience, including me, at least initially, was in his favor. Everyone had something in their mind, cooking up, so that they'd be able to say the right thing at the right time. Nobody wants to be made a fool of in a public space, and everyone's looking for an opening.

Sometimes, debate can be brutal for the losing party. Another guy had something to say as well.

***

"Hi all," he said while putting his hand on a table for support and pushing his legs to stand, drawing the attention of everyone involved in the conversation.

"I am an artist as well. I paint. I'm not half as famous or employed as these guys are," said the other man while pointing his index finger towards the writer. "They have all the movies and shows to write and everything. On the other hand, we are fucked! They have their flowery words and some cash in their pockets. I think creativity just makes you miserable. You get addicted to that misery because it starts to feel good, having a shitty reason for being an absolute mess and engrossed in self-pity every day."

The eyes rolled towards the writer, as people expected a reply. What would the writer say? What reply would the painter have in mind?

A fight seemed likely as more people decided to come closer to the cafe table where the discussion was going on. I forgot to tell you, didn't I? Yeah, I was in a cafe, with a laptop to keep up with appearances. Obviously, writers don't write all the time, but yeah, personally, I have to dig deeper thoughts. It is a mess. You don't want to be there, trust me.

I wasn't able to properly hear what these fellows were discussing. I don't have the enormous confidence needed to join a conversation such as this. My response to most of such shit is, "Man, why do you have to deconstruct everything? Enjoy it as is."

I picked up my chair while being seated and moved closer to them. Yeah, I'm shitty like that. If someone could see me at that moment, they would've thought I'm being glued or something.

A moment of silence prevailed for the writer. There was no comeback from this absolute destruction that the painter inflicted on his opponent. I think he should've seen this coming a long time ago.

"Financial aspect is a subjective aspect, of course. You can't generalize an industry. There are a lot of variables" is what the writer should've said. But he did not, and here he was, discombobulated. He decided to take a breather.

"I can't say you're wrong. I don't have a counter at this time," he said.

"Yeah… because you know I'm right. I'm not saying that you guys have it very easy, but don't you think you guys have it comparatively easier? I mean, grow a spine, man," blurted the painter out of overconfidence. "And also, before you writers date a painter and break his or her heart, remember that we have it much more difficult than you idiots," said the painter, finally putting his ass on the chair.

While most people knew the last part was unnecessary, the victor was clear. But one of the eavesdroppers wasn't particularly ecstatic with this outcome. The man whose face you could say was like a cloud which resembled the face of a clown—get it? Color depends on your preference; I'd say white.

His right hand was slightly longer than his left, for God knows what reason. This man had the expression of a morgue assistant, like he has seen some weird stuff in life. He decided to enter the conversation.

"This guy was definitely going to win," I thought.

"Well… I think you both are wrong. Now, before you start asking about my qualifications to participate in this conversation, I'd like to say I'm a profound thinker who happens to be a prominent playwright and director. I definitely have some significant information to share," this deformed man said.

"I have no story to tell or any poem to recite. I just want to share a theory of mine. I have thought about it a lot and named it the Bubble Theory," said this man. "The Bubble Theory is basically based on human relations, okay? Like, not necessarily romantic relationships but any kind of relationship— our relationship with an ex or tennis or even this earth."

"Cool. Let's hear it," said the writer.

The painter was confident on his higher ground because he was victorious once. Even if he loses, he will have the supposed writer to bully around, like Negroes in chains, being pushed around by the strength that fairer hands had.

***

"Think of your perception of everything as a single color, and the color is unique to you. You're surrounded by it... are born with it, in the form of a bubble of the specified color. If you had the power to see these bubbles, you'd be able to figure out if the color of that item is compatible with you. Changing colors would indicate liars, thieves, manipulators, your wife beaters, and all. And you know, if you stay with this item for long enough, you do see the bubbles and eventually decide to keep up the charade or give up," the man said.

The stuff was getting heavy for these drunkards, but everything they said made sense at that time. Possibly still does; who knows? I was drunk too.

Do we even revisit the thoughts we've had? Yeah, we do, don't we? Yeah, we do. So, there I was intently listening in, and I swear I heard someone clapping. Everything around me faded to black; nothing could be seen. But I could hear voices.

I think the first voice is the supposed writer. He questioned something about the Bubble Theory. Yeah. He asked," What colors might black and white be?"

"I don't really know about white. All colors make up white. So maybe white is everything when clubbed together... all at once. On the other hand, black? What really is black? That's a tough one," said the man.

Meanwhile, I heard a switch in this dark atmosphere. The power was out, it seemed, and soon, I could hear people moving further away from me. I heard whispers, murmurs, among a wave of forced silence.

A cough was as loud as a person dropping on the ground. I looked up and bam! A beam of yellow light blinded me. I couldn't see anything then, either. Here I was, seated in a dark room with a source of light above my head. "Spotlight's not much help," I thought.

"What could the black bubble represent?" I began to think. "The lack of color is black, and so, what lacks everything is black. But what is that thing that has nothing?"

I remember thinking hard about it… and I even got it. It was… what was it? I swear I have it on the tip of my fingers, but motherfucker, I can't find my tongue to say out the letters. Like a loaded gun, itching to push the undigested bullet from its stomach.

Meanwhile, the intensity of the light above my head dropped slowly… and the dark room regained its luminous nature. I saw myself sitting on this chair with a sweater that bore my name.

"The topic of the debate is… 'creativity as the epitome of human existence.' Choose your stands, and the person with the best arguments scores the most points, becoming the winner," said the announcer.

A clock was running in front of the people taking part in the debate. Time. Time has no emotions, no connections, no colors, and no bubbles. But it exists. Something that has the job of pushing other things out of existence exists alongside existence. Fuck.

The black bubble is time.

TEN

A LOVE STORY

My doctor says, "There is a thin, single, solitary, fine line that separates the feeling called love from mindless obsession."

If someone talks to you and gives you some kind of advice, wouldn't you like to see their lips? Well, I never saw this doctor's full face. A different man in white with teeth and lips behind a pale blue cover visits me every day. A lady in white visited me once too, but maybe I was too friendly with her... she never came again. Sad.

Now, my buddies in this treatment center do not agree with the doctors who call me by various names. Demented, twisted, tormented, or even a worthless creature—you can choose either. I think that I do deserve the names imparted to me, but those fuckers handing out these nouns, they're not so "not full of shit" either.

Truth be told, I fucked up big time because I got addicted. Everything is an addiction, first of all. I had this tendency of being hooked on shit since I was a child. First, it was sweets, then cigarettes (that's a nice jump, isn't it), and then pretty much what you can think of.

However, don't you dare think for a minute that I am a loser. I worked for this big research lab as one of the lab assistants, and I was pretty good at what I did. People liked me. I even got to fuck a senior lab researcher once. So, that was pretty neat. We were talking, were alone in the lab, and one thing led to another, and minutes later, her right boob was in my mouth and the left one in the grasp of my hands.

But I digress.

One day, I got hold of the female researcher's laptop after one of our sexual events and declared my love in front of everyone using her blog. The girl had a husband, it turned out, and a boy as well. She had this travel blog where she posted her pictures with the family.

"I'll show you that my love is not foolish or madness like they all publicize. Love just happens, you know," I thought at that time.

So, I drafted an elegant message, stating, "I am in love. I'm in love with this beautiful creature that I met a few months ago. It is powerful and could do anything to survive. I'm in love with this elegant organism."

That was it. The next day, this female researcher comes at me with everything she has got because apparently, the husband was leaving her and taking the child. She slapped the eyes off my face and asked, "Why did you do it?"

"What did I do?" I questioned.

She was visibly upset and pissed. She brought up her right hand and smashed it straight into my left cheek, and man, was I stunned.

"But why?" I screamed.

"You destroyed my marriage! You posted on my blog that you loved me!" the girl said. Perhaps she had hoped that I would say, "Yes! I love you!"

But I digress.

I was agitated for being wrongfully accused. "Woman, fuck you! I was talking about the microorganism that we're working on. Have you seen it? It is unlike any I had ever seen. So beautiful, rare, and the sad truth is, none of you see the potential in it."

A silence settled in the room as the female researcher gave a smile.

"So my life ended because of you, and you didn't even do it voluntarily? What a mess," she said and came closer to me.

"It was fun," she said while bringing her lips towards mine as our breaths mixed up, forming an intoxicating concoction of lustful desires. She brought out her hand and hovered her fingers around my dick as it rose to the point of no return.

I grabbed her neck with my right hand and pushed my left hand inside her pants, grabbing a portion of her left butt cheek—she left out a slight sigh, looking at me with her submissive eyes.

But that was the only action I got that night. She proceeded to knee me in the groin and left the room, saying, "Fuck your microorganism." I think she meant figuratively, but I wouldn't mind if it was literally.

***

Soon after, my private life became a joke in the research lab. The colleagues joked about how I was going mad from the trauma of the loss of my wife and daughter, though I never cared about them. It was just one of those phases in my life that didn't even last that long to make a house in my memories. I don't miss them. I guess I never will.

There were nights when my bitch wife didn't let me sleep, asking me to "help" her with the kid. "Who the hell would then provide for you if I don't sleep well and go to work tomorrow?" I would question. She would just give me a smile, and occasionally, I would even get a one-minute blowjob. But that was all I got.

But I digress.

Well, getting back to the topic. I was working day and night with the head researcher on the microorganism that I was in love with. Have you ever seen a living being under a microscope? They're amazing creatures, man! But my favorite remains this one—which the head researcher classified as a deadly virus.

Isn't it majestic that such a small being can kill millions of people in an instant if it is allowed to?

People have died and gained life forever, and frankly, it is now time for them to realize that they don't matter. Establishing an entire societal order to give their lives meaning that even a small microorganism can take—humans are definitely idiots.

Once again, I digress.

I had never seen such a wonderful microorganism under the lens. I started to feel things I can't explain. I started working with the virus all day.

Every researcher had to wear a protective suit. When the head researcher wasn't around, I would only wear gloves and feel the virus' existence near me. I did not want to damage the delicate being, so I kept a safe distance as well.

The virus is very naughty, you see. It elegantly enters your body, sucks all your happiness, slowly and without failure, until there's nothing left. It is like that one relative that you let into your life, gave them food, and provided them a roof but got berated in front of other relatives by the same person.

I thought that maybe the virus liked to live inside humans. So, I secretly let the virus feed on a few dead bodies, but it seemed to lie dormant inside such bodies. I was under a lot of stress. I guess I just wanted to see the virus work its magic for once, right in front of me. I worked on the virus for about 2 more weeks, and then I decided to plant it on the head researcher.

One Friday, the head researcher asked other people to leave the building earlier and party while asking me to stay with him to work on the virus.

"This is such a fascinating creature, isn't it?" he said.

"I know, right? I thought I was the only one who found it amazing," I replied.

"I want to see it work, though," said the head researcher. "Would you like to be a part of this experimentation? It isn't deadly, believe me."

While I knew the virus was dangerous, if I agreed, I'd be able to see how this virus works. So, I did agree. The head researcher managed a sample of blood, and the virus was allowed to grow inside it.

We both looked patiently at the sample, wondering what will happen when I inject the microorganism inside me. There is a reason why the head researcher and I were obsessed with this creature—it was just beautiful.

Now, as the head researcher was about to inject my beloved virus, I got cold feet.

"Stop. Wait a second. Let me think about it again," I said as he panicked and dropped the injection, spilling the blood everywhere. Coincidentally, this was the only time that the researcher failed to wear the protective suit.

We both got infected, and there is no cure.

Everyone thought I was complacent in my work, and the head researcher testified against me as well. No one believed me, and as a result, I was kicked off the team and forced to go home.

***

The same day, I started having difficulty speaking because of a sore throat. I still have to deal with coughs, fever, and blisters all over. I had medicine, which did not work. The next few days were hell. I would just shit whenever I put strain on my lower body.

A few days passed by, and the supplies in my house were running low. I decided to go out while wearing gloves and other shit. My neighbor met me, and we had a chat.

"Why are you wearing the mask?" the neighbor asked.

"I have the flu," I replied.

"Oh! C'mon, it is just cold. Remove this mask," he said while forcibly snatching the mask from my face. I don't really know why he did that. Maybe because prior to this pandemic, nobody ever gave a shit about masks, gloves, and hygiene.

Not long after, the news of the neighbor and head researcher's dying surfaces, and everybody knows I am the culprit. A big van arrives and drops me here—a kind of concentration camp for the patients of this virus. There is no cure, and we all are projected to die in the coming days. Only the healthy get to live, and we? We get to die in a confined room.

Well, I did fuck a nurse just to get back at them. One day, I even ran away from this institution and came in contact with many people, giving out free hugs to people who need it. I was caught again. The doctors say that I don't have much time, so they might just kill me instead. They accused me of taking at least 20 innocent lives and asked me to give mine in return.

What do they care about? We all are puny, ugly squirrels who can be driven nuts by a simple, single-celled organism. They just feel pain and want to remain in this agony for eons to come.

I am just satisfied with the fact that indeed, the virus did love me back. My love was reciprocated. Now, I shall go and meet my wife. It feels like for an eternity I have waited. Maybe I will tell her all about this virus and how she missed the once-in-a-lifetime opportunity to be loved by a single-celled organism.

ELEVEN

UNEXPLORED?

"Just a few steps and we'll be there," I promised the tourists while I led them to the unexplored fort that lay intact after decades and centuries of abuse from the weather.

I never thought that instead of going to school, I'd have to work to support my parents and do my father's job.

My father was a well-known person in the city, but here, in the outskirts, life is different. My father used to work as a tourist guide, helping all the 'gori ma'ams' and sirs explore the decadent forts that the government has failed to maintain because they have their own fat bellies to fill.

Years passed, and my father got old while the tourism market was filled with younger people who bought houses and turned them into homestays, adventure sports, clubs, cafes, restaurants, and office spaces. For us, the work continued to decrease, and gradually, we started to sell our belongings and lands.

We didn't have much, but we knew the art of getting by. Most of the old-timers who worked as tourist guides gave up their jobs and moved back to their villages, while some started profitable businesses with the money they had saved up.

After I was born, our situation continued to deteriorate, and we decided to move out of our rented place in the main city and found a place to build a 'jhopdi.' On our first night in our new, barely stable home, we could see a strange building that missed our eyes in the morning, which was strange as well.

My father was anything but stupid, and after touring so many forts over the years, he knew it was an ancient one. He ran inside and stumbled around a bit, asking my mother if she had seen a worn-out tube-ish structure that had a piece of glass at the end. She also went inside to help Father find what he was searching for while I wondered why I was unable to see this fort-type structure over the past few years of living in this place.

I was young back then, and my eyes were much better, and I promise you, I saw two people standing outside the fort. The path to the fort was slightly elevated, and when I pinched my eyes to see further, I saw a person on their knees.

A hand crept up on my shoulders, and my father brought out a tube-like structure, which now I understand is called a telescope. He liked to call it the 'yantra' and it was one of the purchases he made to flaunt in front of the 'firangis.'

Father extended the telescope and seemed quite ecstatic. He asked Mother to get his tour bag ready first thing the very next morning and claimed that he 'still got it.'

"Papa, please give me the yantra." I begged, and he said that I could have it for just a second. He extended it to see where the two people I saw went, and there was no sign of them. I did not reach much into this and decided to go to sleep.

My father was ecstatic the next morning and took his cycle towards the railway station. After half an hour, he brought a whole team of 'firangi' with him in a car while his cycle was loaded on the roof. They were going towards the fort.

My father earned a staggering sum that day and returned with an English brand of whiskey along with a saree for my mother and a smaller telescope for me. We all decided to have dinner, and I had to bear 15 minutes of my father blabbering about how good the 'Angrezi' whiskey was.

After he was done with his celebration, he went for the handkerchief in his pocket, only to find out that his telescope was missing, and he never went tour-guiding without it. Inebriated, he decided to travel to the fort and look for the 'yantra.'

Mother objected, but Papa was stubborn when he was drunk. I was too weak and young to intervene back then, and my father took out his cycle and went. The sand kept passing in the hourglass, and around four hours passed, and he did not return. Mother was stressed while I was trying to sleep, but I knew something was wrong.

"Where is he?" repeated my mother every other minute or so, and I was already feeling sleepy as the night had brought sluggishness in my body.

She would never eat without my father. We both continued to wait, worried sick about the man of the house. My mother was more worried about the financial grievances than my father, which did not sit well with me. But she's a woman, and caring for her child is the foremost responsibility.

The sun came up, and Father was still missing. Mother thought that Father could've been robbed, so she went to her brother's house to get help because the police would be of no help for the poor. Mother returned home with my uncle, who said that it was almost dawn and added that they should look for Father once the sun is in full effect.

Nevertheless, Mother insisted, and Uncle sat on his cycle and asked me to look after the barely standing house while he and Mother were away.

I liked him, but it would be the last time I would see either of them. My heart sank as afternoon arrived and the duo was nowhere to be seen. I thought I should go look for them. The sun was shining bright, and the heat was unbearable.

I decided to walk barefoot to the fort because my footwear was with my father. Just a few steps further and a group of 'angrez' in their fancy four-wheeler asked me where my father was.

It was the same group who brought more of their friends, asking me to show them the unexplored palace.

I thought my father would be happy that I brought more customers and decided to take them to the fort. It was my first time traveling in a four-wheeled vehicle, and I had only imagined how they look from the inside. It was quick enough to cover the elevated path in just five minutes.

The gates of the fort were made of iron and were reaching heaven. I could barely see what was beyond that point. Interestingly, the gates were open, and it took all of us to push our way through them.

Upon entering, I saw stairs all around leading to different structures and shouted my mother's and father's names, but no one answered. I kept shouting, and the 'angrez' people that followed me were unbothered. Well, I searched the main area, and I couldn't see anyone until I stepped on a curved instrument.

I fell and hit my head hard. I got up and saw my father's 'yantra,' but he was nowhere to be seen. I keep snooping around to find other clues for my parents' whereabouts but to no avail. The 'angrez' called me out and asked me if I wanted a lift for the way down, and it was getting dark, and I was hungry as well.

I told them if they could spare me something to eat, and they started laughing. They gave me several coins, stating that I earned them, and dropped me home.

Years passed; I was married, and it became my job to take 'angrez' to that fort and back, and I found no evidence of my parents ever being there. I became rich from the tourism business, and soon, your parents were born, who gave birth to you, my beautiful grandchildren.

Each year, thousands of people come to see the unexplored fort, and my store gradually became famous, many people calling the fort haunted. The government closes the gates precisely around 5 PM, and it is opened the next morning at 5 AM.

Well, it's time for my post-dinner walk now; go trouble your father now, shoo! Listen, take this. This is the telescope that I used. This one here is what my father used. I'll give this to you tomorrow!

***

I recall talking to this old man back in '94. It has been a while. I wonder if he is still alive. That night, after reciting his story to the grandchildren, the old man decided to go for a walk.

Upon stepping outside, he recalled the time when the area used to be empty, and now it is filled with houses so close to the fort where his parents vanished. He had always gone inside the fort with dozens of people but never alone at night. So, this time, he decided to take a stroll to the fort.

Upon reaching the gates, the guard immediately recognized him and said, "Mr. Seth, what're you doing this late at night? The gates have been closed."

"Could you slightly open them for me? I want to see the main city from the top of the fort with my telescope. Here, take this money," said the old man.

Mr. Seth went inside the fort, and hours passed; he did not come out, and the guard fell asleep. It was 5 AM, and the guard's duty was about to end. He opened the gates and went inside to check for the old man, only to find a telescope.

He thought the old millionaire would've left when he was asleep and walked away as the next guard resumed his duty.

TWELVE
CYCLING

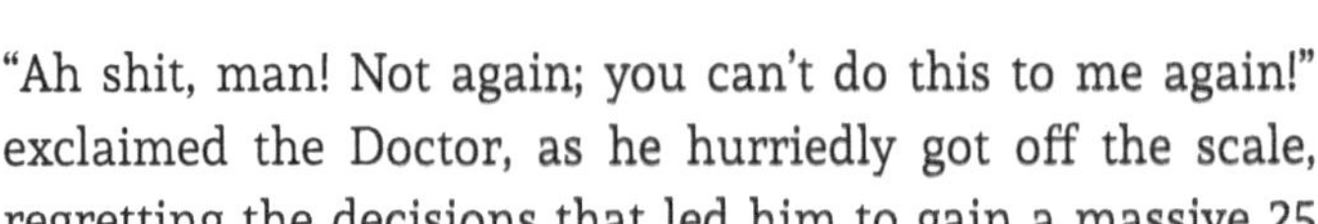

"Ah shit, man! Not again; you can't do this to me again!" exclaimed the Doctor, as he hurriedly got off the scale, regretting the decisions that led him to gain a massive 25 kilograms over the course of the past few months.

He couldn't stand to look at himself—the once handsome doctor, adored by women, loved by ladies, and fantasized by girls—being a fatso. His capable self was now a fraction of his body, which was tired of holding the monumental weight.

"How did this happen? I weighed so little just this August, and since then, I don't think I've eaten much junk," the Doctor thought out loud.

"Is that so?" said a lady who lay on the sofa in front of which the Doctor was standing naked. "You know the only good thing on your body right now? That dick. You've got a good dick, to be honest."

"So, my dick is the only reason you're with me?" the Doctor asked, hovering his index fingers above the tip of his manhood.

"Well, I like many things about you, but if you're getting THIS insecure, don't you think that you should work on your body? Maybe try going out, making love to me, eating healthier shit, man, cutting out the smoothies, and the sugary shit you eat every morning," said the lady.

"Achha Ji? Well, you stuff shit in your mouth with me as well. Yet by some miracle of God, you don't gain a single pound. Same is the case with my wife, who remains the 'too good for me' girl. You're both fucking mean, you know?" said the Doctor.

Well, the lady was visibly upset but continued her attempts to make the Doctor understand the situation.

"You're getting upset. I'm touching a nerve, and you know I'm right. You have a cycle that has been unused for weeks. Last time you had this 'episode of awareness,' you paid six months for a gym that went unused along with this fancy cycle. What is this fascination of yours with expensive shit when cheaper alternatives exist, man?" the lady stressed.

"Well, if you're so troubled by my lifestyle, kindly focus on yours. You're too focused on my bad habits, it seems. Everyone should just start cursing me. It isn't my fault, man—I gave in to my cravings. Fuck me, I committed a sin. Put me in jail," said the Doctor.

"You're turning just into my father, you know? A victim of his surroundings," said the lady. "Do hell with you. Just keep eating and die, you idiot. I don't care anymore."

The lady was hurt and angry with this conversation and went to the bed, not saying or listening to another word. Her angry steps echoed throughout the ground floor of the house while the Doctor decided to visit his 'man cave' and have a beer.

"Even your father is a fatso!" said the Doctor.

The Doctor thought hard while chugging beer like a calf drinking milk from teats. Each sip was followed by a gulp and a little fart on the other end. The process continued for a while as three beer bottles found their way to the dustbin.

"This is such bullshit!" blurted out a slightly drunk and frustrated Doctor.

He started moving towards the stairs and decided to confront the lady, who had been rotating on the bed, waiting for the Doctor to make it up to her. She felt a slight relief upon hearing her lover's footsteps.

The Doctor wasn't always so ignorant and bashful. He had common sense, but the excess of pragmatism and 'not giving a shit' turned him into a robot. Well, it wasn't his fault. He has a difficult past, but so does everyone.

Everybody is sad. Everyone has trauma.

As he approached the room, the Doctor took off his shirt, revealing his bare chest and inflated stomach. He had scars all over his back, like someone dragged him across a road, shirtless, for quite an exhaustive distance. He reached out for the door's handle with his right hand while looking at the time using the watch in his left one. It read 10:36 PM.

As the door opened, the Doctor saw the lady quickly closing her eyes, and he sat down on a chair nearby, opening his shoes and eyeing the lady's reflection in the mirror that stood in front of him. The lady was wearing a comfortable nightgown and slept in a curved position, unaware of her lover's intentions.

"No one would know the benefits of fitness better than me, you know? I'm sorry I was so hard on you earlier. I fucked up, I know. I will start cycling tomorrow; please don't be mad," said the Doctor but received no response.

"Pretty please, I won't do it again, pinky promise," he said, but his repeated statement triggered no reaction from the lady.

He started to move closer towards the lady and stood in front of her face, saying, "You know what I like about you? That you pretend to not give a fuck but keep giving multiple fucks. I'm sorry, please. Now, would you let go? I will take out the cycle tomorrow morning, pinky promise."

"Pinky promise? We don't break those here. Be careful," said the lady warned.

"Pinky promise!" the Doctor said while pouncing on top of the lady. He laid his head on top of hers and played with her hair while she sang a song for him—a song that she had been singing for the Doctor since she joined his clinic as the assistant months ago.

Their affair started not long ago, and the two are now deeply in love. Meanwhile, the Doctor's wife knew about the perverted shit show happening behind her back. So, to sum up, after every such argument, the husband and the mistress would end up having a two-hour sexual act comprising numerous positions while the Doctor would imagine her wife being the one being fucked.

Basically, he wants to win his "fuckability factor" from his wife.

The Doctor loved his wife, but she was too good for him. The wife was fit and fine!

For the wife, her husband was unfuckable until he reduced weight. The moment he started gaining noticeable weight, the wife asked him to find someone else to have sex with. This is a toxic relationship that worked alright until the Doctor decided to start losing weight.

***

Every day, the Doctor started to take his cycle out to his mistress's house, have good sex, and then took lengthy walks. A few weeks in, and the Doctor started losing noticeable weight. The wife would look at her husband going for his walks and cycling sessions daily.

The wife's majority of time was spent in the home gym she had set up a few years ago. Through the windows of her gym space, she would see her husband making progress and gradually started to respect him.

"Here," said the wife, placing a plate filled with mouth-watering chicken dum biryani in front of the husband along with half a bottle of whiskey. "You've been going hard for weeks now. A treat I made for your success. The bitch you've been seeing, ditch her today. I need to get laid. It has been a long time since I've touched it."

The two did end up making love while inebriated, but it was time for the Doctor to break up with the lady, her mistress. The receptionist, however, did love him and couldn't see the Doctor going back to his wife.

The Doctor called the mistress to inform her of his reconciliation with his wife and asked their relationship to be strictly professional.

***

The Doctor made a call.

"I don't wanna fucking hear it," said the lady. "You can't dump me like that. I was the one who gave you a blowjob when you were so deprived of hygiene. Now suddenly, you're this changed man who's all sophisticated and too good for me? In a matter of weeks?"

"You don't have a say," said the wife, while snatching the phone from the husband. "I was the one who allowed this to blossom, and now, I'm the one asking you both to cut this shit out."

The Doctor took the phone back in his hands and placed the device close to his ears while his wife went away to the kitchen.

He saw her wife playing with the knives and cutting fruits with it while the lady argued, "I can't imagine a life without you. Please leave her and come to me, or else I will destroy you. I will file rape charges against you. Don't you hide behind your wife's panties."

"Is she still talking?" asked the wife.

"No," the husband said while cutting the call.

He went towards the kitchen and took the knife from the wife's hand, saying, "You know, I never understood how you can have authority over another human. I mean, I woke up a few months ago, and you said that I wasn't good enough for you. Now suddenly, I am good enough for you. Are you batshit crazy? Fucking cunt! So, whom did you sleep with all this time, huh? Don't tell me you kept your well dried up for months! This was all because you wanted to sleep with someone, wasn't it? This is Rahul's case all over again. Has he returned to your life, huh? Bitch!"

"Oh, so Doctor Drunk is back with a spine now! Go sleep. We'll address this tomorrow. You've come, and I came as well. Why are you fucking this up now? Let's just shut our eyes and figure our relationship out tomorrow, okay cutiepie?" said the lady.

Doctor Drunk dropped the conversation and went away. An eerie silence haunted the house, and the wife wondered where her husband went. She couldn't see her husband but could hear his footsteps all over the house.

The Doctor came back with white hands and took the knife that the wife had kept on the table.

"Why are you wearing gloves? Are you going to the clinic for surgery, or is a patient coming? But you don't see anyone at this hour," questioned a slightly afraid wife.

She began moving away from her husband while he started to move close, slowly. The wife placed both her hands behind her back and started searching for something that would save her life.

"Don't come close to me," said the wife while her hand touched a utensil, then fell, making a loud noise. The wife was startled, and in a moment of weakness, the Drunk Doctor was in front of her, gripping her hip tightly. He slowly started pushing the knife in her wife's stomach, and as soon as she opened her mouth to scream, the Doctor placed two fingers in her mouth to shut her up.

"Is it weird if I'm getting hard now?" questioned the Doctor.

"You fuck!" exclaimed the wife while looking directly into her husband's wife.

The husband continued this back-and-forth movement for a few minutes and wondered, "This knife is my dick now, and we're having sex, aren't we, love?"

Once done, he left the body on the floor and placed his left hand atop his manhood, feeling euphoric.

"What the fuck are you doing? The door was open, so I came in," said the mistress, who decided to talk to the couple face-to-face and find a middle ground.

"I'm so sorry, I fucked up," said the Doctor and started crying while dropping the knife. "I told her that I want to be with you, and she said that she'd kill me if I said that again. In our struggle, I ended her life, and now, I don't know what to do."

"I knew you'd choose me," said the mistress. "You know what! Let's get married and have babies far away from here. Fuck this bitch. Load her in the vehicle; I know what to do with her."

"I'm turned on, you know," said the Doctor. "Okay, let's fuck first."

One of the most satisfying things in life a woman can do for herself is fucking a woman's man in front of the said woman because she hates her guts. The lady got her revenge and now knew that she'd gotten her happily ever after.

"This is kind of a twisted happily ever after, don't you think?" asked the Doctor to the lady whose head rested atop his chest.

The two were looking directly at the wife's body, and a weird thrill ran down their spine again.

"Let's do it again," said the lady while placing her hand on the Doctor's dick. "Somebody's getting hard!"

"We're all twisted in our own ways," said the Doctor while kissing the lady.

Their tongues intertwined, and their breath got heavier with each passing second. The eyes of a dead woman watched as her husband ate his mistress-turned-wife.

THIRTEEN

MISSING DOG

"Bruno! missing for four days," read the poster pasted on a random metal pole next to a magnificent and colorful house in Goa. The pole already had a multitude of other posters of homestays, hostels, and beach cafes and bars, but for Priyesh, this specific poster stood out.

"Rewards guaranteed to the person who finds the dog. The dog was last seen near the beach, asking people to give it a lift. Mind you! The dog is extremely clever and loves traveling on motorcycles. With any information, contact this number!"

The painter stood in the middle of a narrow road with various advertisement boards written in English and Russian but rarely in Hindi or other regional languages. The houses on either side of this lane that led to the beach were huge but stuck to each other—some blue, some green, some blue and green—the houses had their charm. Oh, some houses were yellow too!

This narrow lane had a harrowing existence, occupied by the noise and bustle of the tourist season with occasional moments of silence. Priyesh was still standing in front of the pole, wondering if he had seen the dog somewhere. An eerie peace with the sound of waves in the distance and a stranger looking clueless painted concern in the mind of another dog, which started barking out of the sudden.

"Damn dog, chill," said Priyesh. "I'm looking for this guy, Bruno, right there in the poster. I think I've seen it, but I don't really know where."

The dog whined and sat down, looking with wider eyes at the stranger. The dog then suddenly got up and started to move towards the north while Priyesh remained in front of the pole. The dog started barking, as if asking the tourist to follow him. It took some time for the artist to understand what the dog actually wanted.

As Priyesh started following the dog, the streets once again were occupied by noise as Russians passed by on their modified metal cruisers, laughing and talking about beaches, Indians, and the broader mindset of the people in the country.

"These women are definitely beautiful. If only one could sit on my face, I'd land up in heaven," wondered Priyesh when the dog started barking again. "What? I'm coming!"

The painter continued to follow the dog, and the two took a separate path from the main street and went deeper into the maze of houses near the beach. Priyesh kept following the dog, who would look back at regular intervals to check if the painter was following him or not.

"Yeah, yeah! I'm coming, asshole," said the painter. "I'm sorry. That was unwarranted, but I'm upset, you know. I have my own set of troubles. This is just so random. Why am I following a motherfucking dog?"

The dog stopped, and so did the painter. The canine started barking in front of a yellow and blue house, which had a giant gate and an extremely green yard. Not a single whisper was heard anywhere, and the dog started barking while looking at the house, as if asking the tourist to go inside. The animal would howl and whine, begging Priyesh to go into the house.

"Okay, okay! I'm going inside. Don't yell at me with that adorable face. Well, would you like to come with me?" Priyesh asked.

The dog barked once.

"What is that supposed to mean? Is it a yes? If yes, bark once," said Priyesh.

The dog barked once again, "Woof!"

The painter moved closer towards the gate and felt that the house was quite colder than the others on the main street and rang the bell. No one answered, and the dog and the man waited for a few minutes as the canine's tail wagged slowly, forcing a wave of cold air toward Priyesh's palms.

"I don't think anyone is here, and I definitely don't think that your doggy friend is here," said Priyesh, kneeling down to the level of the dog, who couldn't djigest this judgment and barked a couple of times.

"Okay, okay! Shhh..." said Priyesh nervously and got further close to the gate and peeked through the rods of the metal structure. He could see a man in underwear, swaying his hands in the air, left and right—as if celebrating the loss of the cage of hesitation that mankind has imposed upon itself.

"What the shit?" Priyesh wondered, unable to figure out the situation. "What is this? Some kind of a weird writer's dream where everything is dramatized for entertainment?"

That is true, I must say. You see, this dark empty room, where I pen this story, has its own magnificence. During the day, everything makes sense; there is calmness and a sense of gaiety. However, as the sun sets, I feel loathsome, fearful, as if I'm organizing a deceit against myself. A constant fear that something is coming to get me and is very close, or maybe I manifest it? I really don't know! Well, like everyone on this earth, I face my fears.

So does Priyesh, who pushed the main gate, and to his surprise, the metal behemoth moves away from him. He didn't want the gate to move so that he could return, knowing in his mind that he didn't fall short and tried his best. Now, he was committed, and the issue with us humans is that our pride can push us to do anything, and the painter couldn't show his back to this cause.

Priyesh moved inwards, closer to the main door of the house, where the man was engaged in this weird dance or exercise routine of some sort. It was creepy and sent chills down the painter's spine as he continued to move forward. A weird smell touched the tourist's nose, which seemed to be vile at first, but by passing seconds, Priyesh started to kind of like it.

The man's show stopped, and he turned his head and bare chest, along with those skinny legs, towards the new entrant in the house.

"Hi there," the man said. "Did you know that my son operates one of the boats at the beach and is always the first to find all the big fish—your sharks and all? He makes a shit ton of money, and soon we'll turn this house into a hotel, and we all will retire in some corner of the country, far away from this heat."

"Cool dude. Listen, I wanted to talk about..." Priyesh started to say but was interrupted by the man, who launched a topic of his own.

"You see, my father wasn't a wealthy man, and I had to work hard to build this house. Had my son not assumed the responsibility of the house, the misses and I would've been destroyed. The reason, you ask? Young man I used to drink a lot once, like you, and one day my two-wheeler lost balance on one of these speed breakers, and I damaged something. My son took over and soon got married. Fast forward, they say I'm insane. I think the wife and the son are working to end my life and take over the house. I love them, but I also don't want to die. Don't tell them I said this to you," said the man while getting back to his song and dance.

The wife had heard the mumbling outside and soon came out, asking the tourist if he was lost. "No, I'm not," he said. "I'm not lost, but something else is. This dog, I meant. The dog is lost, and this other dog asked me to follow it, and here I am."

"Come to think of it," said Priyesh, wiping the sweat on his head using his T-shirt, "Now that I say it out loud, this story seems idiotic. I will take your leave."

"Stop!" the wife said. "Don't get any ideas. We know the story that this old man has told you. He has been doing this for a while now. He is a smart but senile man and lives in anxiety constantly, thinking that I am trying to kill him. But that isn't the case. Our son died during a boating accident earlier this year, and since then, my husband hasn't been the same."

"But that doesn't explain the dog. Why did the dog bring me here? Also, he said that you and your son wanted this house?" Priyesh interrogated.

"The current theory is that because this old man trained the dog to bring people to this house so that he can spew this garbage story. You're not the first. All the neighbors have been troubled by this dog," said the lady. "This house, what the old man talked about, has already been mortgaged, and I don't know where we will go once the bank comes knocking."

"Okay. Got it," said the tourist. "I'm so sorry for you. Let me know if I can be of any help. Thank you for entertaining my intrusion in your home and private matters. I am so sorry once again. I will go back."

"Oh no! This is our fault. I am trying to raise funds for my husband's treatment, but nothing is certain," the lady added while putting her hand across the man's shoulder and kissing his head.

Priyesh was a little suspicious because the story seemed too complicated to be real. "But well," he thought, "I tried. Doesn't matter now."

The tourist turned his back towards the house and continued to march outside the gates. The dog, who was waiting for the human, was disappointed and started whining. "Ahh," said Priyesh. "C'mon now, go your own way. Here, take some biscuits. I'm hungry, but I'm giving you these because I think you're hungry. Okay? Now be a good boy and stay here. I'm going. Bbyee!"

The painter left the scene while the dog whined and lay down on his stomach in front of the gate while staring at the wife.

"This isn't right," said the man, pausing his dance number.

The missus stared him in the eyes, turning away, and was back inside the house, in the kitchen, preparing some kind of dish. Meanwhile, the dog could smell meat being cooked inside the four walls and rushed towards the metal gate, trying to force open the game. The canine moved its front paws rapidly, trying to bend the metal but would end up disturbing the sand on the ground's surface.

The woman brought out a rectangular box, put the excess meat in the box, and kept it inside a deep freeze, where similar boxes were stacked, one on top of another.

Meanwhile, Priyesh had reached the main road once again and found a coconut water shop, where he asked the owner, "Sir! There is this house a few meters inside these narrow lanes, yellow and blue in color. It has this huge metal gate and all. What is the story of that place?"

"I don't really know! They are all lunatics. Don't meddle in their affairs. The entire neighborhood was tired of the rowdy son, but after his death, the family has become quite weird and is rarely found outside. A strange stench also comes from their compound. I don't know, sir. They say that the family eats dogs. I don't know. Well, you want coconut?" said the vendor.

"No. I better head back to my hostel. It is quite far from here," said Priyesh while walking towards the bus stop.

FOURTEEN

My Lovely Therapist

"You say you're having weird thoughts. What are they about? I mean... what do you visualize or maybe think about in these "weird thoughts" you talk about?" the therapist questioned.

"I don't really know how to tell you... and honestly, I don't even remember. So, the other night, I swear I got to bed at around 10 PM, after an extremely tiring day, and I decided to doze off. I lay down and started to look at the ceiling. Now, in the place I've rented, the ceiling looks like the inside of a triangle... you know what I mean? Like from the outside, it is one of those triangular structures that you see in beautiful and 'artistic' houses," the patient said while being interrupted by the therapist.

"Gable roofs," she said.

"Huh?" the patient, confused, responded, pulling his eyebrows up.

"They're called gable roofs. The triangular ones. Sorry for interrupting, continue," the therapist said.

"Yeah, whatever. So from the inside, the ceiling is also triangular, and I had switched off the light in my room while switching on the light from the kitchen. A yellow light. This yellow light falls on the left side of this triangular ceiling but not so much on the right side. There are two distinct shades... I still think about them. Well, an astounding 4 hours passed, and here I was, at 2 AM in the morning, looking at my ceiling," added the patient.

"Hmm... interesting. And you say you don't remember anything? C'mon, there must be something from those hours that you can recall," said the therapist while pushing her hair behind her shoulders.

"Hold on. Yes! I do remember that at one point, I was looking at the fan; it was still... I hadn't switched it on. There was dust settled on the edges of the blades, and everything faded away from my periphery, and the only thing I could see was the dust. I think I was brown in color, but maybe it mirrored the blades' color. Is dust transparent?" the patient wondered.

"Are you high by any chance? Not that I will judge or complain to the authorities," she said.

"No, no. I'm sober. That is why I'm here with you. Why do I think about shit like this? Am I even normal?" asked the patient.

"See... I figured out the first problem. Stop thinking that thinking about such things makes you unique. Why? Because this is what I call a dreamy state, where we go to run away from the realities of life, easing some of the pressure that responsibilities put on us. Kind of a self-induced drug...but calling it a 'drug' would be extreme, I guess," replied the therapist.

"Well, when you put it like that, I can't argue. I must say that there is this comfort in that dreamy state. No stress, no loss, just amazement," he said.

"Okay, don't run away to that dreamy state now. We have to address the elephant in the room. Your mother. She has been diagnosed with terminal cancer, right? How does that make you feel? Do you feel sad? Maybe broken? Or something along those lines?" the therapist questioned.

"Now this is the kind of tone, the 'I already know about you' shit one, that I hate! Why, man? Are therapists like these in India or other regions around the globe have such bullshitters too?" a frustrated patient blurted out.

"That was rude and uncalled for! I was trying to help you reach the conclusion faster so that you wouldn't have to spend more money on these sessions," she cleared.

"Okay. Truce! During the initial days of the diagnosis, I felt nothing. I mean, I didn't know what to feel. People should cry, feel sad, or maybe bang their head against the wall. I didn't really have a clue... still don't. One fine day, Ma' said that she wouldn't die before seeing my child's face, and that made me tear up a little bit. I never really thought that I had limited time with her, you see. But I'm making my peace with it, just like my mother did. She said that she'll be one of those rare cases that beats terminal cancer. She is a warrior," the patient added.

"That's nice. You should learn a thing or two from her," the therapist said.

The patient turned his face towards the window, once again lost in his own thoughts. The therapist's office was on the second floor of a rundown building that had "paan" stains at all the wall intersections. Even the staircase wasn't able to stop the spitters. It seemed like a few people had peed on the stairs as well... an unbearable stench protruded through the nostrils of all those who visited the therapist.

"I have... a lot. Over the years. Well, is it me, or are we really making good progress? I think we're definitely done for the day!" continued the patient while turning his face towards the therapist out of the blue.

"We still have about half an hour. Here's what I will tell you about you from the conversation we had so that you start to take me seriously! First, you have strong deflection tendencies... you easily lose your train of thought. Second, you are very defensive when I try to bring up topics that you don't like to discuss. Third, you are intelligent, but you think that you're at the top. You cannot be your own therapist. You want more? 'Cause I can go on and on!" a frustrated therapist said.

"I won't argue on that," said the patient. "And I won't call your bluff. What more would you like to ask?

"Tell me about your day. What do you do, apart from coming here and taking my personal time, despite my requests to schedule for morning slots?" she said while adjusting her spectacles and writing something in her neatly maintained file.

"I sleep at around 2 or 3 AM, then make my own breakfast, work, get ready for my workout, come back, make my dinner, and sleep. It is the days when I'm free that shake my mind. I go to the beach, swim, and everything... yet I can't shake these weird thoughts. It is like I live an entire movie in this 'dreamy state.' The weekends are the worst. I wish they never came, you know. So much time and nothing to do," said the patient.

"What about women? Do you have a girlfriend? When was the last time you had sex?" asked the therapist.

"Ah! Now you're asking the right questions. Being a woman yourself, why don't you tell me what you all motherfucking want? I mean, you all just have unreal expectations and are so fucking reserved all the time? No one is out to hurt you; at least smile when a person smiles while looking at you," he said.

"You have strong opinions when it comes to women, don't you?" asked the therapist.

"Well, it would be a lot easier if women could just say and know what they want. I mean, do they expect us to come to them only to be rejected? There is always some guy or the other that has fucked a woman's head, and so she can't be engaged in a romantic involvement. Don't be engaged romantically, but you can have sex, can't you? For pleasure? Like a HUMAN," the patient said.

"It is much more complex than that, trust me. Life is not all butterflies for women. You know how many people hit on a girl on a daily basis? Well, we are getting off the topic here. I concur that you haven't gotten laid in a long time," she said while putting her right leg on top of her left one.

"I tried for a while. Even those women that like me didn't want to move ahead because of some shitty reason or another, or I think that they just wanted to talk and pass their time using me," said the patient.

"You attract what you are," said the therapist.

"I'm not a person who'd string along another human just because I have no better person to pass time with," said the patient.

"You would," countered the therapist.

"That's true. I would," accepted the patient.

The patient once again turned his head and started looking towards the window. An aircraft was visible in the sky, and much closer to the eyes were the birds. Faint noise of honking and a traffic jam was also audible. He lost himself in the hubbub for a while and closed his eyes, interlocking his fingers and putting his hand on his stomach.

"It is crazy, no? I mean, this entire conversation, I could very well create in my head and solve my own anxiety and stress via self-dissection. Any person wouldn't need a therapist if they would just look inside their messy minds. I think I'm already cured...maybe this shit is working for me. I know I have my flaws, ma'am, and I'm also working on them. There is nothing in this world that I would love more than being more complete...so that I don't have to depend on others for calmness again. I think if this day had arrived earlier, maybe I could've cleared my head a lot faster," said the patient.

"You're awfully quiet," he said again while opening his eyes and found the seat in front of him empty. "The fuck? Where are you? Ma'am? Therapist, madame? Miss-know-all?"

"Damn! Was I in the 'dreamy' state? For how long? What the fuck?" a panicked patient wondered.

He got up immediately and decided to snoop around to clear his head of the confusion regarding his own existence.

"This doesn't look like my home at all. Where am I? Was I stoned?" weird thoughts started pouring into the patient's head again.

Suddenly, a strange unlocking sound was heard from a corner of the room. It was the entrance to the room, and the door opened as the therapist walked in.

"Where were you?" a panicked patient said.

"Do you think I have only one patient? Another one was waiting, so I sent them to my main room. This is the room reserved for one-time clients," said the therapist.

"One-time client?" asked the patient.

"Yeah! You are not mentally ill or depressed or anything like that. You are fully functional and have good emotional intelligence. The only thing wrong with you is your overthinking. You think a lot, and most of the shit is garbage...most of it will only land you in trouble. Be calm...don't overthink... just roll with life," advised the therapist.

"But..." replied the patient.

"No! There are many patients that need much better care and deserve my time. You are not broken; there is nothing wrong with you. You are not unique. The reality is you are sound, just like any other person—crushing your own happiness by constantly contemplating why you aren't content," the therapist concluded.

FIFTEEN

PAHAAD

Note: This story is written in Hindi language using English letters. The intention was to make you work for this story because... why not? I'm the fucking writer!

Ek Monday aya, aur mai office mei apne laptop kei keyboard pei emotionless kuch type kiye ja raha tha. Tabhi "Mountains are calling," bolkar mera colleague Rishabh mere peeth par apne haathon ki chaap chor gya. Kareeb 20 logon ka plan hai, pahadon mein jaake party karne ka, aur mujhe bhi offer aya hai.

"Pahad?" waha pei kya hoga, maine Rishabh se bola. "Shanti," usne mujhse kaha.

Kaisi shanti? Yeh 20 logg sasti daaru leke, apni mehengi maa-baap ki gaadiyon mei pahadon mei jaake halla hi toh kareinge. Toh faida kya iss do kaudi ki shanti ka. Faida kya iss dikhavati jeevan ka jaha salary paatey hi udha dena hota hai aur social media pei show off karna hota hai? Kya inn logon mei sharam nahi hai, ya yeh itney andhakar mei jeerhey hai ki inko yeh nahi samajh ata ki agar daaru hi amrit hota, toh Mahadev ko Neelkanth nahi kaha jaata.

Khair idea acha tha, maine saal ki shuruat se chutti nahi li thi aur ab shayad thodey din pahadon mein jaakey shanti mei rehne se mujhe accha hi lagta. Lekin ek problem thi, mere paas car thi nahi aur inn logon kei sath mujhe jaana nahi tha. Toh ab bike rent karni thi aur ek badiya shaant si jagah dhundhni thi, par kaha?

Ek website pei bahot dhundhne par mujhe mila ek homestay, jiskey 18 reviews the aur main road se kareeb 2 ghante ki chadhai pei tha. Aur price? Matra 250 rupai per day. Bataao. Aur kya chahiye tha mujhe jeevan mei. Maine 5 din ki booking karli aur bike renting company se ek sasti scooty ki baat bhi ho gayi.

***

Abhi trip shuru honey mei 3 din the aur mere colleagues mujhse puchte ki tumko nahi chalna? Maine saaf mana kardiya, kehkar ki bahot kaam hai mere par. "Tum saaley promotion leke hi manogey kya," Rishabh bola. Mai ek ghatiya si muskurahat ke sath, iss taney ko mann mein pees kar wapis laptop pei khit phit karne laga. Lekin main toh mera ab bhi aaney wale 5 dino pei tha, woh arram kei din jaha mere alawa agar koi hoga bhi, toh shayad mere hi jaisa ho. Akhir mujhe bhi toh pata chaley ki mere jaise log khush kaise rehte hai apne jeevan mai?

Packing maine pehle hi shuru kardi thi, ek raincoat, ek pani ki bottle jisme mai raste bhar paani bharta chalunga, kuch garam kapde, aur chappal.

Mujhe meetha bahot pasand hai isliye meine khoob chocolate bhi rakhli. Thursday ko main office gaya. Apni workspace se uthkar mai coffee lene gya aur tabhi Rishabh aata hai aur mujhse kehta hai, "Sarthak bhai last time puch raha hun, chalega?" Maine baat ghuma diya, kyuki mujhe naa kehna nahi aata.

Ek atyant sundar gaali deke Rishabh chala gya aur main phir apne laptop mein lag gaya. Baat yeh hai ki Rishabh ko trip pei jaana hai kyuki Muskan jaa rahi hai, uski office crush. Bahut time se laga hua hai banda usko apni taraf akarshit karne mein pyar woh hai ki abhi toh bhav deti hai par uska mann hava se bhi jaldi disha badal leta hai. Disha se yaad aya, mai kabhi kabhi sochta hun ki office ki Disha kya mujhe pasand karti hogi?

Agar woh jaati toh shayad mai bhi chala jaata par uskey boyfriend aur uska Goa ka plan bana hua hai mutual dosto ke sath. Khair mujhe kya, "Mountains were calling me," soch kar mai wapis kaam mei laggya.

***

Akhir woh din aa hi gaya, bike maine ek raat pehle hi utha li thi aur ab, samaan baandh kar safar kei liye mai taiyyar tha. Subah kei 4 baje the aur mai apne PG kei bahar bike start karkey ready hogya. 8 ghante ka safar tha maximum 2 baje tak toh pahuch hi jaunga maine socha.

Dheere dheere karkey mai aage badhta gaya aur meri khushi ka thikana nahi tha.

Zindagi ka rasta seedha kiska hota hai, kabhi tedha kabhi medha, aur kabhi gol-gol. Mujhe lagta hai ki bachpan ka rasta sabse sidha hota hai aur slowly elevation badh jaata hai aur ham kuttonn jaaise apni hi puch kei peeche gol-gol daudhkar thak jaatey hai. Kyu? Kyuki humko yeh nahi pata hota hai ki jis shanti ki hum talash mein hai woh toh bilkul humare peeche hi hai lekin hum hi aagey bhag bhag kei apni life ko kho dete hai.

Khair, meelon ki doori tai karkey, mujhe pahad dikhne lagey. Door se toh bahut khoobsoorat lagte hai woh aur agar unki kokh mein jao, toh ek shanti hoti hai, jo suraj kei neeche jaatey jaatey daravni hojati hai. Kuch aur 100 kilometer jaakey, mujhe main road se ek turn mila. Main road jati thi ek mandir ki or, ek devta ka mandir. Aur usi modh par ek dukaan thi, jaha maine socha thoda rest karte hai.

"Bhai yeh batao, yeh mandir kis devta ka hai," maine chai wale se pucha.

"Sahab mai toh yaha naya hi hun, jiski ek dukaan hai woh toh seher mei rehta hai aur mai wahin se aya hun. Kehte hai iss mandir ki bahot manyata hai aur agar aap yaha aaye ho, toh kuch paise, bhaley hi ek rupai, chadha dena chahiye, isse woh devta apni raksha karte hai," chaiwaley nei bola.

Mujhe laga ab iske baad woh mujhe prasad aur foolon ki maala bechne ki koshish karega aur isliye mai usko chai kei paise deke main road se upar jaa rahi patli sadak ki or nikal gya. Google dikha rha tha ki udhar hi tha homestay.

Bada hi ajjeb sa rasta tha, na kachi sadak thi na pakki aur poorey raste koi insaan nahi tha. Raste mei bas khub saare girgit the. Aisa lag raha tha ki sab mujhe hi dekh rahe hai. Maine gaadi nahi roki. Ek choti pahadi kei around gol-gol raston se woh sadak bani thi aur jitna mai upar jaun, road utni hi kharaab hoti jaaye.

Thoda upar jaane pei mujhe kai ghar dikhayi diye, jinmei koi rehta nahi tha aur taaley lage the. Aisa lagta tha ki koi aake sabko bhaga gaya ho. Lekin Google abhi aur upar jaane ko keh raha tha.

Maine darr kei maare homestay wale ko phone kiya aur poocha, ki kya rasta sahi hai. Usne bola, "tum aate jao, hum tumko dekh paa rahe hai." Meri jaan mein jaan ayi aur mai aur upar sadak pei jaane laga.

Dheere dheere sadak poori pathreeli ho gyi aur ek jagah meri scooty atak gyi. Jaise hi mai neeche utra dhakka dekar gaadi nikalne ko, beesiyon girgit apne bil se bahar aagye, mai turant upar chadha aur poora throttle deke kisi tarah vahan se bhaga. Mere aage badhte hi, ek mota sa patthar peeche gir gya, aur mere wapas lautne ka rasta ho gya block.

Upar ek surang thi, poori khuli aur andheri, koi bhi andar ja sakta tha, aisa andhera jaise maano sooraj ko koi jeev nigal gya ho. Surang dekh k lagta tha ki use blast karke banaya gaya tha. Waha pe bahut purani machines, tractor, aur construction ka samaan bhi pada tha. Aur lagta tha ki saalon se kaam band pada ho.

Maine jyada dhyan nahi diya aur upar nikal gaya. Mujhe ek ghar dikhai dene laga. Waha pei teen logg khadey mera intezaar karr rahe the. Unhoney mera naam le k chillaya, "sahi aa rahe ho, aate jao."

***

Jin pahadon ki mohabbat kei peeche mai itna door aagya, kya woh utne khoobsurat samne se bhi the or was I delusional?

Apni bhadey pei li bike se maine samaan nikala aur homestay mei jaakey rakh diya. Kuch alag hi mahaul tha waha, ajeeb se darvaze jo band honey ka naam nahi lete the aur ek 14 saal ka kutta, jo abhi bhi 3 saal ka dikhta tha. Homestay ka malik tha Rajveer aur meri kismat dekho, Rajveer kei ek dost ka naam bhi Rishabh tha aur doosri ek ladki, Drishti. Hi hello karne kei baad, hum tayyar ho gye lunch ke liye. Bhookh toh bahot zoron ki lagi thi aur khane mein tha dal bhaat, the staple food of every person from North India.

Humne khana shuru kiya aur ek ajeeb sa sannata cha gya, or awkward silence, as we used to call it in the corporate world. "Kuch toh bol bhai, aise kya saadhu ban kar baitha hai," maine socha.

"Toh Rishabh aap kya karte ho?" maine pucha.

Usne ek muskaan dekar bola mai bhi tumhari hi tarah ek corporate slave tha, phir maine sab chor diya aur ab kai mahinon se issi homestay pei hun. Drishti ki bhi same hi story thi aur Rajveer nei toh jaise chuppi hi saadh rakhi thi. Maine socha ki kitna rude aadmi hai yeh, apne guest se kuch baat hi nahi karta. Khair, lunch karke itni zor neend aayi maano koi meeting chal rahi ho. Mai so gya.

Kuch der baad koi halchal si hui, ek madhur si dhun sunai de rahi thi par aisa lag raha tha ki mai abhi sapne mei hun. 5 minute toh mujhe uthne mei lag gye aur phir samajh aya yeh mera alarm tha joki mujhe office se nikalne ka indication deta tha. Meri hasi choot gyi aur mai neeche dinner ka haal chaal lene chala gya. Waha mujhe Rajveer dikha dinner banate, usne mujhe dekha aur pucha, "Anda curry chalegi?"

"Mujhe kuch bhi chalega," maine usko bola.

"Mera ek dost tha, issi elakey mein aaya tha ghumne," Rajveer ney bola. "Usko kisi ne bataya hoga iss mandir kei barey mei aur woh daudta daudta aagya idhar. Ek number ka ghumakkad tha."

"Woh jab aaya toh bahot zoor ki barish ho rahi thi toh neeche main road ki dukaan waley nei usko upar jane ko bola, issi ghar mei. Tab yeh homestay nahi hua karta tha, bas ek ghar tha joki shayad ussi dukaan waley ka tha."

Maine tok tei huye pucha, "Ek minute! Kya yeh aap ka ghar nahi hai?"

"Nahi nahi, maine lease pei liya hai kuch saalon kei liye," Rajveer bola. "Toh jo mera dost tha, woh idhar aakey ruka raat bhar aur nikal jaane ka socha. Woh raste mei jaa hi raha tha ki two turn kei baad, road mein uski bike fas gayi aur barish ki wajah se udhar landslide aa gayi aur uspe patthar gir gya."

"On the spot death is what you'd call it," Rajveer said.

Mujhe phir mere alarm ki awaz aane lagi, mai gya wapis kamre mei aur apne alarm ko band kiya. "Yeh saala alarm ne mera jeena haram kar rakha hai," maine socha aur phir neeche bhaga, Rajveer ki kahani poori sun nei. Par woh waha tha nahi, aise gayab hogya tha ki jaise hava kei anei sei badal.

"Rajveer?" maine uska naam pukara aur tab samne aa gayi Disha.

"You're looking for Rajveer? Woh neeche gya hai, surang side kisi kaam se," Disha said.

"Toh mohtarma, aap yaha kaise ayi?" maine Disha se pucha.

Muskura kar usne kaha "Mai West Bengal se hu, yaha pei cheap rate key wajah se aayi thi. Meri ek dost thi jo yaha pehle aa chuki thi apne trekker boyfriend ke sath. Dono ko trek karne ka bada shauk tha. Aap yahan se upar jaoge na, jungle kei raste se chadhkar, toh pahad ke uss paar ek bahot sunder bugyal hai. Wahi karne ko aye the woh dono lekin on the way, barish aagyi and dono ki fisal kar death hogyi thi."

"So sad, kya naam tha aap ki uss dost ka?" maine pucha hi tha tab tak phir se alarm bajne laga. "Ek second mein aaya," bolkar mai gya alarm band karne. Maine apne phone ke repeated alarms off kiye aur phone hi switch off kardiya. Phir mai wapis gya toh raste mei hi Rishabh khada tha.

"Toh bhai app yaha kaise aye?" maine usse pucha.

"Mai Disha kei sath aya tha, woh meri girlfriend hai and hum dono upar Bugyal ki trek karne aaye hai." Rishabh nei kaha.

Mai thoda confused toh tha but ittefak samjh kar mai Rajeev and Disha ko kitchen mai dhundhne gaya kyunki dinner ka time ho rha tha.

Rishabh aur Disha nei mujhse pucha, "Kal aap bugyal chalogey?" aur wahi Rajveer nei mujhse kaha, "Kal yaar woh surang explore karne chalte hai."

Mujhe thoda ajeeb laga yeh sab. Phir maine bola, "jab dinner hojaye, toh batana" aur mai apne kamre mei chala gya.

***

Kamre kei raste mein ek reception type area tha waha ek table pei entry book thi. Book khuli thi toh maine socha dekh lu ki kitne logg aatey hai iss homestay mei. Mujhe sirf teen hi entry dikhai di, Rajveer, Disha, aur Rishabh ki woh bhi mahino key antaral mei. Mai peeche muda toh woh teeno mere peeche khase ghoore jaa rahe the, aisa maano ki mere andar tak jhaank rahey ho. Maine dinner kei barey mei pucha, unhone kuch bola nahi bas ghoorte rahe. Phir mai unki side se nikal kar andhere mei bike ki oor gaya toh dekha woh teeno mere peeche hi aa rhe the.

"Kya hua? Kuch chahiye?" maine bola.

Saare milkar hasne lage aur bole, "It's a prank bro, chill! Hum tmko jhoothi kahaniyon se dara rahe the aur tumhari shakal dekhne wali thi."

Khair agla din aaya, aur hum chaaro ne decide kiya ki hum surang dekhne jainge. Subah sabne torches rakhi apne bags mei. Excitement sabke chehre par dikh rahi thi.

***

Surang kei bahar ek board tha peele rang ka jismei kaale aksharon se likha tha ki yaha pei entry sakht mana hai. Gufa kei aas paas kaafi patthar gira hua tha aur Disha, Rajveer, aur Rishabh chalte chalte kaafi age aa gye the. "Yaar yeh Sarthak nahi dikh raha," Disha nei Rajveer se bola.

Rishabh nei kaha, "Yaar woh shayad peeche reh gya, mai jaakey dekhu kya? Kahin naraz toh nahi hai?"

"Chodh na bhai, aa jayega. Waise bhi phattu hai," Rajveer bola.

"Arey woh dekho, aage ek bike padi hui hai," Disha chillai. "Kisi ka accident ho gaya hai!"

Uss bike ka peela number plate tha, matlab rented thi. Rajveer thoda agey badh aur signal dhundne ki koshish karne lagaa taaki ambulance ya police koi mil jaaye. Teeno ne dekha ki kuch khoon nei nishan surang ki oor jaa rahe the. Jab unhone torch maari toh surang mei ek sher dikha jo jis aadmi ka accident hua tha uska peit cheer kei kha raha tha.

Disha, Rajveer, aur Rishabh teeno statue ho gye. "Rishabh, woh body dekhi hui lag rahi hai. Yaar uski shakal jaani pehchani si lag rahi hai!" Disha boli.

Rishabh bola, "Shant reh, sabko marwayegi kya. Dheere dheere ghar ki oor chal!"

Utne mai Rajveer bolta,"Rishabh, Drishti, yaar woh toh uss bandey ki body hai jo kal apne paas aaya tha, Sarthak!"

Jo bhi ho, mera manana yeh hai ki pahad door se jitne khoodsurat dikhte hai, paas se utne hi rahasyamayi ho jaate hain. Din ke ujale mei suljhe lagte pahad, raat mei bhut anjaane ho jaate hai.